NEXT OF KIN

A Novella

by
ROD COLLINS

Editing, layout and cover design by solfire@phoenix-farm.com

ISBN: 9781726824040

STYLE NOTE: the usage of numbers as symbols throughout this novella was a deliberate choice reflecting police reports and the quick nature when running through thoughts and clues. Blame my editor if this style choice goes against your training. She has agreed to take all the heat for this cop-talk choice.

Dedicated to
my wife
and the Vista Grande Library's
Inklings Writers Group

who encouraged me, critiqued
me and sometimes gently pushed
me.

Thanks!

CHAPTER 1

He checked his watch — 3:15 in the afternoon. Only 15 minutes from the time he targeted. But precision was not needed on this job.

Everyone thinks that evenings, nights or early mornings are the best time for this type of operation. Sneak in, then out. Undetected. Mission completed. But this assassin was highly trained. First by Uncle Sam, but mostly by notorious experts he sought out and paid for additional knowledge over the past 6 years. Stakeouts and intelligence gathering were high on his list of acquired skills.

The back yard was large. The house sat on several acres, as all the upscale houses in this neighborhood did. There were trees, bushes and flowers scattered about the yard with hedges around the perimeter. All vegetation needed to block off gazes from the neighbors, and to also block prying eyes from his presence. On the rear deck was a large grill, a good-sized custom built bar, hot tub and assorted patio furniture.

He made his way across the yard and settled in behind a planted fern. From there someone would have to be within 10 feet to see him. Looking through the back door window he could view the next important item on this mission.

He checked his watch — 4:10.

Any time now.

He heard a car coming up the driveway. Car doors slammed, a female voice said something indistinguishable. The first family member, the daughter, now home. The sound of the car backing down the driveway came next and he kept his eyes focused through the back window.

The red light on the back door monitor turned off and he quickly picked the back door lock and was in. A few seconds later the light came back on showing that the house security system was back on.

The daughter had gone upstairs to her room. He heard her footsteps running up the stairs. She was not his first thought though. Silently he moved through the kitchen to the door to the garage. Slipping in he used a pen light to do a search and quickly found what he was expecting.

Back into the kitchen; he heard music coming from the second floor. He made his way up the stairs and down the hall. The door was open where the music was coming from. A quick peek in confirmed the teenager was not present. A light appeared from under a door at the back of the room. He moved close. A toilet flushed and the door was pulled open from the inside.

She stopped cold. Eyes wide. Mouth open. She never said a word as the aluminum baseball bat came down on her head. *One down,* he said to himself.

He made his way back downstairs to the kitchen and checked his watch again. The next victims would come through the garage.

In 15 minutes the garage door opened and he heard a car pulling in. Eighteen-year-old Burt was now home from high school. The garage door closed then a car door opened and closed. Burt entered the kitchen and almost made it to the refrigerator before his head shattered and his world blacked out forever.

One more to go.

Mom arrived 20 minutes later, right on time. She parked in the driveway behind Burt's car in the garage. She had her own garage door remote and always came into the house through the garage/kitchen door. Usually she was carrying some groceries and it was more convenient to bring them right into the kitchen. When she entered she stopped and wondered which one of her kids had spilled ketchup on the floor. Her question was cut short forever by the assassin behind her.

He looked around and made sure he had not stepped in any of the blood now creeping across the kitchen floor. Dusk was settling over the landscape outside and shortly it would be dark enough to exit safely.

He went out the kitchen/garage door and closed it behind him. His gloved hand placed the bat up against the door. Over at Burt's car he found the garage remote. He pushed it once, then when the door was halfway up, pushed it again and the door started down.

He quickly rolled under the closing door and was invisible as he made his way down the edge of the driveway to the street. Ripping off his paper jumpsuit, he transformed into one of the nondescript joggers that frequented these suburban roads. A few minutes later he was in his car and leaving the area.

At 8:30 that evening the man of the house, the breadwinner, loving father and husband waited in the driveway as the garage door slowly went up. He pulled into his spot next to Burt's car and close to the door. He grabbed his briefcase from the seat beside him and walked the few steps to the kitchen door. *Who left this here?* he thought as he picked up the bat. Grabbing it, he came into the kitchen and tossed his briefcase on the nearest counter. Walking across the kitchen, still holding the bat, he realized that he was stepping in something sticky on the floor. He looked down, and then followed the trail to his wife.

CHAPTER 2

The bodies in the kitchen were covered when Detective Jim Bodine Harrick arrived. Detective Harrick could have obscurely fit in anywhere. Nothing about his plain appearance and JC Penny sport coat said *cop* except for the slight bulge on his right hip from his Sig P239. He was 45 years old, average height at 6' 1", 230 or so pounds, some of that carried noticeably around the waist. He did have most of his hair; brown that was just starting to show streaks and tints of gray.

The Michigan State Police officers and medical examiner were upstairs with the daughter. Mr. Barnes was sitting in the living room with his head in his hands sobbing. Two Grand Ledge uniformed officers were standing nearby, keeping a sour eye on him. Homicides were rare in this small town west of Lansing and 3 in a single night was record making.

Harrick entered and noticed the security alarm pad just inside the door. He stopped for a second and looked right looking into the living room. *The husband,* he surmised. He did not go far down the hallway knowing that the forensic specialist still had work to do. One of the state police troopers gave him a quick glance and then nodded toward upstairs.

Harrick saw Detective Green of the Grand Ledge Police Department standing in the upstairs hallway looking into a room. Green looked over at his counterpart and acknowledged him. "Hey, Jimbo, welcome to the slaughterhouse."

Jim stopped and stared at Green. Green suddenly remembered that Detective Harrick hated that nickname and made sure everyone knew it.

"Sorry, Jim," Green said. "It's been a while. Thought you retired."

"No, 2 alimonies and 2 kids in college won't let me. What ya got?"

"Coroner is in here," pointing inside the room. "Amanda Barnes, 15, skull cracked open."

Harrick peeked around the doorframe and looked inside. The body of a young girl was on the floor. Medical technicians were performing all the required tests on her.

"The others are downstairs," Green added. "Eighteen year old Burt Barnes and Barnes' wife Kristine, both dead, both with their heads bashed in."

"Husband?" Harrick asked.

"He called it in. Says he got home about 8:30 and discovered the bodies. Call came into us at 8:47. What he did for 15 minutes, no one knows."

Green shrugged in true puzzlement then continued. "He has blood all over him and we found what we believe is the murder weapon, an aluminum baseball bat. It has blood on it. Your state people will be testing it to make sure."

"Anything from your department on threats or anything suspicious toward the family?" Harrick asked.

"No, nothing. I checked that already. We're talking to the neighbors but they can't think of any problems."

Detective Harrick shrugged and went back downstairs. A state police captain had arrived and instructed his troopers and Harrick to take Mr. Barnes in for more questioning.

CHAPTER 3

I t was past 3a.m. when Harrick finally rolled into his bed. The interrogation had gone on for several hours. Barnes stuck to his story the whole time. He swore he came home late as usual and discovered the bodies. First his wife, then his son. He said he then just lost it; screaming, crying and yelling, not believing this had happened. Then he said he thought about his daughter and ran through the house looking for her. After he found her in her bedroom, he fell apart again. Finally he got it together enough to call 911.

Harrick asked about the bat. It had been tested by then and found to be the murder weapon. Barnes' fingerprints were all over it. Barnes said he found it by the garage door and thought one of his kids had left it there. The investigators pressed him: if someone had broken in and killed his family, why was nothing else missing, as in a robbery, and why was the house alarm still set? Barnes didn't know. When he opened the front door as the first officers arrived, he had not shut off the alarm. The security company then notified the Grand Ledge Police about the alarm.

Ya, probably the husband, he thought as he fell asleep.

The assassin was also just getting home and would be asleep soon.

~ ~ ~

Det. Jim Harrick spent his early years in the army serving in the military police. The last 4 years of his 10 years of service were spent as an instructor, then chief instructor for new MP recruits. As such he was more than adequate in firearms and hand-to-hand combat. His hand-to-hand skills were not the "for show" type as taught by most karate schools, but actual what he used to call, "Take a drunk, fighting young infantry kid and have him cry for mommy."

One of the tricks he was known for was to have new trainees handcuff him, do a standard search on him and then transport him to another location. All were clueless when they opened the back car door and reached in to haul him out. The usual scenario was that his right hand caught the second trainee in the solar plexus, sending the newbie to the ground gasping for air. Then a quick arm/neck grab and twist on the closest other one and that trainee was on the ground with Jim holding the kid's service pistol pointed at their face.

What they did not know, and most never got the privilege to know, was that Sergeant Harrick had been given a small tool, passed on from his father when he was in the military police. A slim tool with a standard handcuff key on one end and a small, razor sharp ½" blade on the other, protected by a plastic cap. The slim device fit securely behind a rigged belt in the small of his back.

CHAPTER 4

Jim woke up a little past 8 in the morning. He put a pod in his Keurig and waited as the one serving of coffee filled his mug. He then found his phone, sat down at the small kitchen table and dialed his boss.

"Morning Jim, late night I heard," Captain Meyers said.

"Morning Captain. Ya great hours I have," Jim replied.

"Don't complain to me. You turned down a 9 to 5 office job several years back." Meyers had a chuckle in his voice.

"I couldn't put up with the politics and other bullshit that came with it. I'll stick to the street. I thought I would go down to Mr. Barnes' place of employment this morning," Jim responded. He was sure his boss would have anticipated that but Meyers was good to work with, leaving him alone on his own schedule, well most of the time anyway. Meyers respected Jim and knew he was good at his job so Jim liked to keep the communications clear as a sign of respect.

"Okay, then swing by the coroner's office, they may have time of deaths established."

"Fine, I'll keep you updated." Jim disconnected.

At 8:30 he had finished his shower and was downing a bowl of crunchy Chex when his phone rang. "Hi Pop," the familiar voice said.

Amy Hamilton, 21, was his step-daughter from his second wife. The marriage lasted 8 years, a little longer than marriage number 1. Amy loved Jim and was disappointed in her mom that she let a good guy go just to have an affair with her dentist. That broke up 2 marriages, and 2 families. Her mom was somewhere in Texas.

Amy had been 12 when Jim married her mom. Jim was the father figure she needed. There were a few teenage disagreements (No, you can't go on a date at 15 with a senior in your high school!) but it all worked out. She always called him Dad or more often, "Pops". Amy had an interest in science, so Jim would tell her many stories of how science helped solve various crimes.

She enrolled in Michigan State University part-time and Jim was able to get her working part-time at the Michigan State Police as a researcher/computer whiz/gofer. This helped pay for college, which he supplemented.

It was April, spring break, so she was working full-time and in the office now.

"Hi kid, what's up?"

"Heard you caught a triple last night. Anything juicy?"

"No, just starting to explore."

"The news is saying this morning it was really gruesome, saying the father is a suspect."

"Well, we don't know much yet. I'm sure you'll hack into the department's computer to read the coroner's report."

"Dad!"

"That's okay kid, I know you won't blabber mouth. Listen, I got to get going so will see you later. Love you."

CHAPTER 5

Harrick checked his notes from the previous night and drove over to Barnes' place of employment. Wayward Financial was located in a 4 story office building in East Lansing. Looking at the directory in the lobby, Wayward occupied the top 2 floors. He caught an elevator and hit the 4 button. *Might as well start at the top,* he thought.

Harrick stepped off the elevator and saw a receptionist at a desk in front of him. He walked over, took out his badge and ID, then asked to speak to whoever was in charge.

The well-dressed woman behind the desk never looked up. "What does this concern?" she asked.

"It concerns a detective from the Michigan State Police wanting to see someone in charge." Harrick was firm, but polite.

She looked up quickly, and saw the gold badge. "Oh, sorry."

Jim smiled.

The receptionist picked up her phone and punched in 3 digits. "Mr. Williams, there is a detective from the state police here to see you, a Mr..." She looked up at him with a questioning expression.

"Harrick, Detective Harrick."

She repeated the name into the phone.

"One moment Detective Harrick. Mr. Williams, the senior partner will be right out."

In a few minutes a tall, late fiftyish gentleman came down the hall and extended a hand to Harrick. His professional demeanor did not hide his obvious concern. "Detective Harrick? I'm Terry Williams, senior partner here. I probably know why you're here. Let's go back to my office."

Williams led him to a corner office with a nice view of the Michigan State University campus. Once he closed the door, Williams pointed to a large leather chair opposite his desk. Harrick sat and pulled out his note pad and pen.

"We heard about Ted, *eh*, Mr. Barnes, on the news this morning. Just terrible. We are all in shock here. Mr. Barnes was a nice guy, liked by everyone. I assume that's why you're here?"

"What did Barnes do here? What is Wayward Financial?" Harrick asked.

"We offer several financial services. Some are to individuals but mostly small companies and small municipalities. We manage and invest pensions, retirement accounts, investments, and so forth. Mr. Barnes worked a floor below us as an accountant."

"Did Barnes work alone?"

"No, we have a dozen or so accountants here and they mostly work as a team."

"Mostly?" The word piqued his interest.

"Some of our more experienced and trusted ones manage some individual accounts. Mr. Barnes was one of those."

"Did any of those individuals express concerns about how Mr. Barnes was doing?"

"Not that I'm aware of. I talked to Greg Hughes, the senior accountant and manager of that section this morning. I asked him the same thing. Greg said that all of Barnes' individual accounts are doing extremely well. We've started an audit on his accounts just in case."

Harrick reached into his pocket and handed Williams one of his cards. Williams responded with his own.

"I would like to talk to your HR person and Mr. Hughes if I could."

"Of course, they're both on the third floor. HR is on the left when you step off the elevator and Accounting is down the hall on the right. I'll call ahead so they'll be expecting you."

They exchanged a few more questions and answers then Harrick rose. "If you think of anything else please call me."

Williams rose to escort him but Harrick held up his hand, "I can find my way. Thanks!"

Harrick stepped off on the third floor and looked both ways. *HR first.*

He easily found the correct door and walked in. The room was split into 2 main sections; the front section, where a secretary sat, showed an open door to a nicer office for the HR director.

A lady in her mid-thirties came out of the inner office and extended her hand. "Detective Harrick?, I'm Janet Casteel. Please come in."

Harrick entered and Ms. Casteel closed the door behind them. Harrick showed his identification and they both sat down in her spacious and well-furnished office.

She spoke first. "I have pulled Mr. Barnes' employment file. What would you like to know?"

"How long has Mr. Barnes worked here?"

"Let's see," she opened the folder and paused for a moment, "5 years this says."

"That's not long. Where did he work before?'

"*Hmm,*" she continued to look through the paperwork. "Says here that he owned his own accounting firm up in Cadillac. There is a note recommending his employment here by Greg Hughes."

"Any complaints, any disciplinary actions on Barnes?"

"Nothing in the file, and it would be in here if there was."

Harrick leaned forward, "Anything in the wind, office scuttlebutt, water fountain talk?"

"Nothing. And I do hear the gossip here, but no, nothing on him."

"Thanks." Harrick handed her his card and rose. "I would like a copy of his personnel file."

"Let me clear it with legal, but it should be no problem."

CHAPTER 6

He left the HR office and walked past the elevator to Accounting. Unlike HR, Accounting sprawled over most of the rest of that floor. He entered and saw about a dozen offices around the perimeter and a dozen or so cubicles running down the center. A receptionist saw him come in and immediately was on the phone.

"Mr. Hughes, the detective is here."

Mr. Hughes was shorter than Harrick; many inches shorter than the standard bar of 6 feet. He was probably middle forties and carried an extra 50 pounds. Balding and with thick glasses he looked like . . . well . . . an accountant.

Hughes guided him back to his office.

"Detective," Hughes started, "we all can't believe this. I know Ted personally and there isn't a nicer guy in the world."

Harrick got out his notepad. "Barnes said he worked late last night. Did anyone see him or is anyone able to confirm this?"

"We have several people who like to work late. I'll collect some names and get them to you. Plus, our parking lot has 24 hour cameras. They should show when he left."

"Did you notice any attitude changes recently with him? Anything bothering him lately that you would know of?"

"No, nothing. Our kids go to the same school and my son is on the baseball team with his. We meet socially every so often. The news is saying he's a suspect. I just can't believe that."

"Drugs or alcohol?"

"No, Ted was a social drinker, maybe a couple glasses of wine if we were out to dinner together. I have never seen him drunk or high."

"HR said he started just a few years ago here; that you recommended him. What's the story behind that?"

"Ted called me up about 5 years ago. We had been college roommates -- I hadn't heard from him in several years but then he called and asked if there were positions open here. He said he was selling his business in Cadillac and wanted to relocate back to the Lansing area for better schools. I knew he was smart and knew his stuff. We worked together several times in college, so I recommended him. He started here and took right off, doing some outstanding work."

"Mr. Williams said he also managed some individual accounts. Any problems there?"

"No. Even though we were good friends I still had oversight on those accounts. They're performing very well. We're doing an audit, per Mr. William's instructions, on those accounts, but I would bet my house there's nothing bad going on."

"Okay, thanks." Harrick again handed out his card. "If you think of anything, no matter how minor, please let me know. Also let me know the result of your audit."

CHAPTER 7

Detective Harrick drove down Michigan Ave. toward Lansing. It was noon and he was tempted to stop at Kewpee's for an olive cheeseburger. But parking would be a pain this time of day, so he drove on to the coroner's office.

The staff was eating lunch in the break room near the examining room. The county coroner noticed him, put down his Hardees burger, and waved him in. "Hey, Jim! I heard you caught this."

"Hey doc, ya know anything?"

They went over to the exam room, where 3 tables were occupied, covered in sheets.

The doctor went to the first table and lifted the sheet. "Sally Barnes, age 15. A single blow to the head. Hit from the front. Probably died instantly. Wound fits the aluminum bat found at the scene. She was probably the first."

"About what time?" Harrick asked.

"Oh, we're saying about 4pm give or take half an hour."

They walked over to the middle table.

"Burt Barnes," the doc mentioned as he pulled back the sheet. "Age 18. Again blows to the head, but this time from behind."

"Time?"

"We think not too much later than the daughter. Maybe a half hour later."

They moved to the third table.

"Mrs. Barnes, same thing. Blows to the head from that same bat. Could have been up to an hour after the first one."

"Any defensive wounds?"

"None," the doc replied. "Seems all were caught by surprise."

"Report?"

"Maybe a week."

"Okay, send it over when done."

Jim headed back over to his office. He called Amy on her work phone. "What's up Pops?"

"Amy, need your help."

"As usual," Amy interjected.

"Wayward Financial has parking lot cameras. See if you can download from yesterday morning to midnight. Mr. Williams at Wayward can authorize. And no hacking! We need permission."

"What we looking for?"

"Mr. Barnes' red Lexus sedan."

"On it!"

CHAPTER 8

The assassin was just waking up. It was 9a.m. on Friday morning and the outside temperature was slowly climbing past 60 degrees. He had taken his time driving, making sure he drove straight home and wouldn't stand out to any police that might have been out last night. When he got home late Thursday, he had parked his 4 year old Ford Focus in the large garage. The lights were on in the house, thanks to timers on various lights. His Toyota 4X4 was still parked next to the side door.

He lived on one of the many small lakes just outside of Cadillac, on property he inherited from his parents. There were neighbors, but the lots were large when developed back in the 1940s and mature trees surrounded most of the older cabins. He had added new insulation, fixed up the inside and added the garage many years back. This was to be a home for his family. The house was set back about 75 feet from the shoreline. A dock extended 20 feet into the lake where a small aluminum boat was secured.

He had acquaintances at work and sometimes would join them for beer and pizza at the bar near work. He never invited anyone to his home. There was just one person he would call a close friend, which was okay. The co-workers knew the pain he was going through and they didn't try to force themselves into his life. "He'll come along in time," they had commented to each other.

His job as a firefighter and paramedic gave him the time off he needed for his missions — 5 days on, living at the station, then 3 days off. Rotating time on/time off like this all year long, year after year. Anyone on the firehouse squad who needed an extra day or more off, for a vacation or such, would switch and cover each other's shifts. His days off this week-Wednesday, Thursday and Friday- would end tomorrow. The job also helped keep him in top physical shape. The station had a nice workout area and his fellow professionals made it a daily routine to practice and keep in shape.

He made coffee and walked out on his back porch. He sat in the wooden rocker his wife used to love and blew on the hot beverage to cool it. Staring out onto the calm waters of the lake, he thought about the last 5 years.

Almost done, he thought.

CHAPTER 9

H arrick spent the weekend as he usually did. First, Saturday was locked in for helping his local lodge with their pancake breakfast. He was in charge of bacon. About 11am, after cleanup, he returned home and changed into faded jeans and an old MSU t-shirt. He grabbed a Vernors ginger ale out of the fridge and went into his garage. Turning on the lights highlighted a car hidden under a large tarp. Pulling the tarp off revealed a classic 1956 Studebaker Goldenhawk. He bought this car when he was just 17 — at a time when it was not considered a classic. With its dents, sticky transmission and oil burning engine, it was very cheap transportation. Over the last decades he had been slowly restoring it back to original condition. Only a few Goldenhawks in original shape existed in the whole country. One of the others was in Jay Leno's garage.

Finding the correct parts was difficult.

Remanufactured ones would not do for a purist like Jim. Most of the parts were from other respected collectors. They exchanged lists of what they were looking for. When Jim went out scavenging old junkyards, barns, warehouses, etc., he kept a lookout for them. A few times he bought parts off EBay. Once, about a year ago, he was taken for several hundred dollars on a part advertised as original but which was obviously a reproduction. The well-established seller was adamant that Harrick "didn't know shit" and refused to give a refund. A few weeks later Harrick heard that the seller was hacked and all his personal information, including his Social Security number, credit card numbers, bank accounts and such, ended up on the dark web. Harrick thought about asking Amy if she and her computer geek friends at MSU knew anything about this, but after considering a bit, he decided he didn't want to put her in a position to possibly lie to him.

There was little work left to do and today he was buffing out the new paint. Nine months ago he was digging through an old automotive repair and paint shop from the 60's in Detroit with his scavenger friends. Most of his friends came up disappointed but he found gold in several cans of original paint, in the original color. He negotiated a fair price with the family of the long deceased shop owner and dropped the paint off at his painter.

Harrick had almost lost the car in his first divorce. The car was considered community property and his wife's attorney at the time wanted the car sold and profits split. He knew the divorce was mostly his fault. Few wives understood the life of a cop. The long days, shifting hours and constant worry took its toll.

Harrick offered to buy out her share of the car but the appraisal came in several thousand dollars more than he could come up with. He was forced to take out a high interest loan that had him eating Kraft mac & cheese for several years. But that was a long time ago and he and the car survived. Their son Rick was now attending Ohio State University. Harrick believed that the main reason Rick chose Ohio State was because of the fierce rivalry between his own alma mater, Michigan State University, and that jock college in Columbus. Just one more jab at his dad. Harrick's cool relationship with Rick was justly deserved due to his many absences as a father. Being a cop was his life, he once wrongly thought.

He was a lot smarter with his second marriage, insisting on a pre-nup. The second wife disappeared anyway so the car was not an issue. The one good part of the second marriage was his step-daughter Amy.

Harrick acknowledged that he was not very good at marriage. Yet, given a chance, circumstances might roll around so that he could be as good a father to his son as he tried to be to Amy.

CHAPTER 10

It was Monday morning; Harrick arrived at his office a little after 8am. He opened his computer and checked his messages. He had a follow-up message from the lab, on an unsolved murder from December. The gun matched the bullet pulled from a drug dealer killed on Washington Ave. The gun came off another drug dealer arrested last week in a sweep. Harrick would inform the state district attorney, who would probably call the Lansing DA and they would all schedule a sit down with the arrested gun holder and his attorney. Some compromise offer would be made other than life in prison. Maybe 15 to 25. After all, he did get rid of another drug dealer. With him serving his time in Jackson Prison that would take 2 bad guys off the streets.

The other messages did not intrigue him. He opened some files on his computer and spent the morning reviewing some older cases assigned to him.

At 10am he called Amy.

Amy picked up on the second ring. "Yeah Pops!?"

"Hey kid. Do you have the tapes from Wayward Financial?"

"The lab techs just brought them in a half hour ago. We're going through them now. Probably be early afternoon before we have anything."

"Okay. Thanks. Let me know as soon as you can." Harrick hung up.

Harrick looked up Mr. Williams' number and gave him a call. A pleasant-sounding lady answered.

"Mr. Williams' office."

"Hi, this is Detective Harrick from the Michigan State Police. Is Mr. Williams in?"

"One moment please."

About ten seconds later, Mr. Williams came on the line. "Hello detective, how can I help?"

"Did you find people there who saw Mr. Barnes on Thursday evening?"

"Yes," Williams replied. "We have 3 people who said they saw Barnes in his office until a little after 6pm that day. Also, about a dozen people saw him there from early morning, about 8 and through the day. He did leave at about 11:30 to have lunch with a client. One of our sales people, James Kirby, went with them. James said they were back a little after 1."

"Please email that list to me. I'd like to interview them at your offices this afternoon if you don't mind."

"I'd like you to be discreet. We have clients in from time to time. I can have an office provided where you can have some privacy."

"That would be fine Mr. Williams. I appreciate your cooperation."

"Well, the more we find out about the timeline, it just looks like he didn't do it," Williams added.

"We'll see."

CHAPTER 11

After lunch Harrick drove out to Wayward Financial. He had the list of employees from Mr. Williams. From 1pm to 3pm, he talked to each one, making notes in his small notebook as each told their recollections. They all closely agreed on when Mr. Barnes arrived that morning, when he went to lunch and returned, and when he left. The closely agreed times were noteworthy. If they all were conspiring to provide Barnes an alibi then they all would be telling the same exact timeframe. Yet, they were sometimes off 15 minutes or so in what they remembered, but never enough time for Barnes to drive home, kill his family, then return.

He interviewed James Kirby. Kirby provided the name of the restaurant and the client they entertained for lunch.

"No," Kirby said, "Ted didn't seem worried, nervous or anything else out of the ordinary. He was real happy and upbeat the whole time."

On his way out of Wayward Financial, Harrick checked his iPhone. There was a single word message from Amy time-stamped a half hour ago.

"Done."

Harrick drove over to the lab, arriving about a quarter to 4. He walked in and signed the check-in sheet. The front desk officer looked up and acknowledged him. "Hey Jim."

"Hey Joe."

"How's the car?"

"Getting done."

They'd been doing this for years.

He walked back to the lab offices where the department's main computer was housed. Amy had a desk here but was usually away somewhere else doing the odd jobs assigned to her. He did find her close by, hovering over a couple of other lab geeks looking at a large computer screen.

"Pops, come look."

He walked over and stared at the screen. On the screen was a video of a parking garage entrance. The time clock was moving but nothing was happening. "Okay?"

The senior lab tech was sitting at the computer. He didn't mind that Harrick would many times bypass him and go straight to his daughter for requests. Amy would always keep him up-to-date and in the loop. He hoped that after she graduated she would stay on full-time. The senior tech spoke up after a few more seconds of watching the monitor. "This is a true copy of the garage tape from Wayward on Thursday. The time stamps are correct."

The tech typed on the keyboard and the tape on the screen went into fast reverse. "At 7:55am we see Mr. Barnes' red Lexus enter the garage. The license plate is pretty clear."

He fast forwarded the tape. "At 11:35 we see the car exiting. You can see a driver and a passenger. The driver is definitely Mr. Barnes. The passenger is not identified as yet."

"Mr. James Kirby," Harrick added.

"Amy," the tech said, "please note that Detective Harrick identified the passenger as a Mr. James Kirby." After receiving a nod from her, the tech continued, "We see the car return at 1:10pm. Then leave again at 7:55." The tech looked up at Harrick.

"But there's more!" Amy enthusiastically chimed in.

"Yes," the tech responded. He typed on the keyboard. Another video came up. "They also had cameras in the lobby. These confirm Mr. Barnes' movements and times that we saw on the other tape."

Harrick was writing in his notebook. He was realizing that this information just put him back to square one. "No hurry on the report."

"As soon as Amy types it up, I'll sign it and send you a PDF."

CHAPTER 12

The next 2 weeks were unfruitful. By then, all the reports were in. No other prints were found in the house or on the murder weapon. Nothing was stolen. The neighbors heard nothing. No signs of forced entry. *A professional?* Harrick thought. *Barnes in trouble somehow from his old job in Cadillac?* That didn't make sense either.

Why kill the family and not Barnes?

Harrick had interviewed Barnes again a week after the crime. Ted Barnes looked 20 years older than last week. His eyes were red, face drawn; he looked in pain. Not physical pain but mental pain. The life was drained out of him. Barnes, with his attorney present, did not have anything to add. Harrick told them about the people in his office and video that corroborated his alibi. Barnes insisted he did not know of any enemies, had not received any threats and had no idea who could have done this. The funerals for his family were coming up in a few days. Harrick could see that Barnes was going through hell,and felt sad for him.

Harrick was at his desk reviewing reports of another crime when his phone rang. Captain Meyers was on the other end. "My office," he said and hung up.

He entered Meyers' office and closed the door. A young state trooper was standing off to the side. Harrick did not recognize him. "Detective Jim Harrick, Trooper Bill Grayson," Meyers said.

Harrick and Grayson shook hands.

"Trooper Grayson is from the Cadillac post," Meyers explained. "He's down here to testify in a state case and heard about the Barnes murders. He may have something interesting."

Harrick and Grayson sat down.

Grayson spoke, "Yours sounds like the same MO we had up in Cadillac a few years ago. Fellow came home from work and found his family dead. A real brutal scene I heard. Anyway, the county took over the crime scene. The father was the prime but no charges were ever filed."

"You remember the name?" Harrick asked.

"Stan or Stanley Lisowski."

"Anything else come to mind?"

"Nope, that's it. Just thinking the strange circumstances matched your homicides," Grayson said.

The captain spoke up, "Barnes has a connection to Cadillac doesn't he? Run with it Harrick."

"Yupper Captain, and thanks Grayson. Stay safe out there."

Grayson nodded and Harrick went back to his desk. *What does that tell me?* he asked himself.

A few different ideas went through his head. After contemplating for 20 minutes he called the senior tech at the lab. "I need Amy for a day for some research please," he asked.

"Yeah, I can spare her. One of your cases?"

"The Barnes murders."

"I'll transfer you over."

"Hi Pops!"

"Amy I need your magical research skills. Senior said I can have you for a day."

"What do you need?"

Harrick explained the recent conversation with Trooper Grayson. "Check on the Lisowski murders. Ask for a copy of the files from the county. Also see if there are other family murders like Barnes and Lisowski in Michigan."

"On it!" Amy replied. She sounded cheerful, even though it was tedious work. She truly loved this part of crime fighting.

CHAPTER 13

Amy's report was in his inbox the next morning. He printed it off, read and reread it, occasionally making notes on the pages. After an hour he picked up his phone and dialed an extension. "You free Captain?" He always was for Harrick so Jim headed down the hall right away.

Captain Meyers motioned Harrick into his office. Harrick sat. He had Amy's report in his hands. "What you got?" the captain inquired.

"I had Amy do some research for me yesterday. She got the files for the Lisowski murders up in Cadillac. Killer there used a golf club, one from a set that belonged to Mr. Stan Lisowski. Wife and 3 kids clubbed to death. Mr. Lisowski found them. Everything else looks the same as Barnes.

Middle of the day, no forced entry, nothing stolen. The county sheriff is heading up the case but he's made no arrests as yet."

"She," the captain interrupted.

"What?"

"She, the sheriff there is a she."

"What happened to Sheriff Potter? When I was up in the Gaylord Post he'd been the main man there for many years. Unbeatable in elections. Did he retire?"

"Better than that. Won 4.5 million in the lottery 4 years ago. Quit that same month, packed up and now owns a bar on a skimpy bikini beach in St. Thomas."

"Damn lucky bastard!" Harrick sighed.

"New sheriff there is Elinor Starr. Doing a good job I'm told. She was re-elected last year. But back to your report."

"What also came up is that these 2 are not the only ones. There's a third."

The captain leaned forward. This was getting interesting.

"Antonio Garcia, age 41, civil rights attorney in Southfield. Almost 2 years ago. His whole family slaughtered in their house. Wife and three children ages 14, 10 and 8. Southfield PD has the case. Still unsolved. They have cleared Mr. Garcia."

"Years apart." The captain said deep in thought. "What do these 3 have in common?"

"Not a clue."

"Find out."

CHAPTER 14

Southfield, Michigan, was over an hour's drive from Lansing by way of I-96/696. Harrick called Southfield PD to set up an appointment the next day with the investigator from the Southfield Police Department and their district attorney assigned to the case.

In the morning, he drove his personal car, a 2-year-old Camry, to the office and worked on some other cases. His appointment was at 1pm, so he didn't have to leave until 11:00 or so. That would give him time for a quick bite to eat. He drove over to the motor pool about 10:30 and checked out a silver unmarked Chevy Impala police vehicle. These cars came with a big engine and with an upgraded suspension that gave them a nice ride.

He pulled onto I-496 East. Just past East Lansing merged onto I-96. He set the cruise control on 70, just under the limit. No hurry. There was plenty of time.

The 3 cases tumbled over in his head. Two had ties to Cadillac. One didn't as far as he knew now. He needed to pursue a Cadillac connection with the Southfield investigators.

The day was sunny and warm. The miles clipped by in a melodic rhythm. It was a pleasant drive so far.

At the Howell exit, about half way into his trip, a large car hauler slowly passed him on the left. What first caught his attention were the classic cars on the trailer. *Someone is moving them to Detroit,* he thought. A pristine 1963 Corvette Sting Ray was on the front top. A 1969 Dodge Charger on the front bottom. Also a Mustang, Harrick didn't know the year of this one from a glance. A Camaro, and on last sat a 1956 Studebaker Goldenhawk.

A very familiar-looking 1956 Studebacker Goldenhawk.

Harrick was stunned for a moment. *Can't be.* He toggled the police radio in the car and connected with the Lansing State Police Post. He identified himself, asking that they contact Delta Township Police and have them drive by his home.

Harrick took the car off cruise control and sped up to keep pace a couple hundred feet behind the car hauler. 15 minutes later he got the call back from the Lansing Post. Garage door open, alarm bypassed . . . and no car.

As they approached Brighton, Harrick radioed the Brighton Post. Sooner than he expected, 2 blue state police cars and a weighmaster car had pulled up with him. *Good idea, the weighmaster can pull him over to check loads and bills of lading, no probable cause needed.*

The weighmaster's vehicle sped up and lit up the trailer. The trailer slowed down and pulled over onto the right shoulder. The weighmaster and state police blue units pulled in behind.

Harrick pulled in behind all the other vehicles and stayed in his car. The troopers knew why they were there and it would be better to let them do their job. On the radio he heard one trooper say he was going to check the VINs while the weighmaster interviewed the driver.

After about 15 minutes a trooper walked back to Harrick's car. "Yeah, it's yours alright. The VIN matches. All of them have been reported stolen or will be reported soon, I suspect. You got lucky."

"The driver?" Harrick asked.

"Don't know nothing. Says he was hired yesterday to drive them to Detroit. Cars were already loaded when he showed up at a truck stop in Lansing."

Harrick was sure that the driver would be questioned intensely back at the Brighton Post. Maybe the story would change, maybe not.

"Afraid we will have to impound them for a while. You want the bust?" the trooper added.

"No, you guys get the collar." Harrick gave him his card and asked to be kept informed. Professional courtesy in the ranks, plus the fact that they would get the credit for stopping a half million dollar theft, would assure he'd get his car back at the earliest possible date and in pristine condition.

CHAPTER 15

The delay with his stolen car meant that lunch would have to be fast food. Harrick found a McDonalds a few miles from the Southfield Police Station. In the drive through he ordered the fish filet combo, no pickle. *What sick mind thought of putting pickles on a fish sandwich?* He parked in the lot of the police station and ate his meal. At 5 minutes to 1 he got out of his car, brushed the salt from the fries off his sports coat, and entered the building.

At the metal detector he showed his ID and badge then was waved around the sensors; 2 pounds of a loaded Sig p239 plus a pair of handcuffs would make those alarms scream. He again identified himself to the receptionist and was directed to the second floor. "Turn right off the elevators," he was told, "and Detective Baxter's office is 2 doors down."

The door to Detective Baxter's office was open yet Harrick gave a polite tap on the door as he entered. An African American man in his 40s was behind the desk. Wearing a white shirt and tie, his suit jacket was hanging from a coat rack in the corner. He rose when Harrick entered. A Glock 25 in a DeSantis holster was visible on his belt. A second man in a suit was sitting beside the desk. He was Caucasian, mid-thirties, taller by about 5 inches and 30 pounds leaner than Baxter.

"Welcome Detective Harrick." Baxter extended his hand. "This is Jim Carr, Assistant DA."

Harrick shook hands with both men and sat down in a chair near the others.

Baxter started the conversation, "Frankly I am surprised it took you so long to get ahold of us."

Harrick was momentarily puzzled. "You are?"

"Yes." Baxter explained. "When we heard about your murders in Grand Ledge we contacted the State Police Inter Agency Support Section, with a report on our murders. Must have been 2 weeks ago."

Damn, Harrick thought. *Another inter office message screw up.*

"I appreciate you sending that over. It's just hasn't reached my desk yet." Harrick needed to bring this up with his captain when he got back. "What can you tell me about the Garcia case?"

"I made a full copy of our file," Baxter said while handing Harrick a stuffed file folder. They both opened their files and Baxter continued. "On August 20th, 2015, a friend stopped by the Garcia house to pick up one of the kids. The friend, Christina Perez, said that was about 4pm. She said she usually picked up the Garcia daughter to take her and her own daughter to dance classes. Nobody answered and Ms. Perez went around the back and looked in the windows. She saw Mrs. Garcia on the floor in a pool of blood. Perez tried the back door but it was locked. She ran back to her car and called 911. The police arrived in 10 minutes, forcefully entered the house and found 4 dead. Mrs. Garcia, age 34, Christina, age 14, Veronica, age 10 and Joseph age 8. Coroner said they had been dead at least a couple of hours. Mr. Garcia was in court in Detroit all that day."

"Any signs of forced entry?" Harrick asked.

"None."

"Sexual assaults?"

"None."

"Any history of drugs?"

Again none.

"Did Mr. Garcia have any enemies?"

"That's the hard part." That statement prompted a puzzled look so Jim Carr explained, "He has lots of people who don't like him. Everyone knew he was going to be a big pain in the butt when he showed up. Usually he worked on immigrants' rights cases and minorities issues. Several liberal foundations are paying his wages. I've gone up against him several times in court. He's very good, a fierce advocate, and makes a very good living. And yes, he is a pain in the ass."

Harrick skimmed through the rest of the folder. What he wanted to know wasn't here. "Did you set up the appointment I requested with him?" Harrick asked.

"Yup. He said he would be in his office all afternoon and we can stop over."

Baxter rose, put on his perfectly pressed jacket and grabbed a set of keys from his desk. "I'll drive."

Jim Carr bowed out of the trip. "Keep me informed of anything new you may find out," he requested.

Antonio Garcia's office building was just a few minutes away. It was about half past 2 when they entered a very lavish outer office where the receptionist sat. She dialed a number, talked a few seconds, then rose and escorted them back to Garcia's office.

Mr. Garcia's office was also very well decorated. Fine, handcrafted walnut bookcases extended along most of the wall behind a large desk. Mr. Garcia was on the phone. He was dressed in an expensive custom-tailored black suit. *The kind of suit that would cost me a third of my annual wages.* Garcia held his hand up, pointing one finger to signify just a minute and motioned Harrick and Baxter to 2 plush leather chairs in the office corner.

Garcia ended his conversation and joined them. "Good afternoon Detective Baxter. Any news?"

They all shook hands as the introductions went around. "Mr. Garcia, this is Detective Harrick from the Michigan State Police. He would like to ask you some questions."

"Mr. Garcia," Harrick said. "First, I am very sorry for your loss. I can't imagine the pain you've gone through."

"Thank you Detective," Garcia said mournfully. "I heard there was another family murder like mine in Grand Ledge a couple of weeks ago. Any leads there?"

"Sorry, can't say much about that one. Have you thought about that day, that time in your life, more over the past year? Any new information that comes to mind?"

"No, nothing. I haven't a clue in the world. For the life of me I don't know anyone who could have done it."

"Have you had any cases or dealings in Cadillac or the surrounding area in the past?"

Garcia looked confused. "Cadillac? No, never even been there."

"Anybody from Cadillac you may have had dealings with? Does the name Stanley Lisowski ring a bell?"

"No, again, I have had no connection with anyone at or from there. Is this important? Is he a suspect?"

"No. The family in our other case had just moved down from Cadillac. We were wondering if there was any connection. We have to look at many possibilities." Harrick did not want to bring up the third family murder.

Harrick rose and gave Garcia his card. "If you think of anything, please let us know." Garcia nodded absently as they left.

CHAPTER 16

After talking to Garcia, Harrick had Baxter swing over to Garcia's house. Garcia no longer lived there, having moved into an apartment soon after the murders.

"The house is still on the market," Baxter explained. "They have lowered the price several times, but the idea of a triple homicide there has scared buyers off."

They drove into a nice subdivision with large expensive homes on large lots. Garcia's house was a 2-story brick colonial with a 3-car attached garage. An older FOR SALE sign from a realtor was in the front yard.

"Price is down to $325,000. That should be a 450 to 500 thousand dollar house in this market."

They parked the car in the driveway and exited. Harrick stood there for a moment taking in the whole picture. Expansive yard, mature trees, lots of professional landscaping, lots of places out front where someone could hide.

Baxter motioned toward the door. "Want to come in? Mr. Garcia gave me a key."

"Not just yet," Harrick replied. "I want to do a walk around."

Harrick walked up to the garage and looked through the small windows. Not much to see in there. He turned right and went around the corner to the south side. Again there was an abundance of well-maintained landscaping. Bushes trimmed and some flower beds along the side. A set of concrete pavers made a walkway from the driveway along this side of the house.

There was a tall wooden fence with a gate at the back. The fence looked like it went around the whole back yard. Harrick tried the latch to the gate and it opened. He stepped through and found concrete pavers now extending to the left to the back yard.

The back yard was huge. *Has to be at least a full acre.* Mature maple trees marked the property line in the back 5 feet in front of the fence. A half dozen more maple trees were planted in various spots around the yard.

Harrick walked up to a large elevated wooden deck that covered a good 20 by 30 feet. Stepping up onto the deck he noticed a pool and hot tub accessible off the back. *Civil rights must pay well*, he presumed.

He heard a door slide open behind him. Harrick turned and saw Baxter leaning out the door. "Yah, easy to sneak in from the back and not be seen by neighbors," Baxter commented.

Harrick nodded. "Let's see the inside."

For the next hour Baxter led him through the house. Baxter gave him the most likely sequence of events as they went from room to room. They ended up back in the kitchen where the last murder took place.

"The cleanup people did a good job," Harrick said.

"Professional service, although they tore up and replaced the carpet in the kid's room and family room," Baxter replied.

Family, Harrick thought. He imagined the family living, breathing, here. They're having dinner, planning vacations, watching TV together. *A family*, he thought again. Then, without warning, in an instant, destroyed. *I should have worked better at my own family. But . . . Amy. Another chance. Again, God keeps trying to teach me that as doors close, others open.*

"I noticed no alarm."

"They had only been living here a few months. The house is wired but they didn't have a service as yet. Mr. Garcia said he was going to get a service contracted but had not gotten around to it. Just another thing that still bothers him a lot. Anything else?"

Harrick looked around then paused for a second before answering. "No, I'm good. Thanks."

The drive back to Lansing was quiet. Again he asked himself, *What do I now know?* His self didn't respond. It was as confused as ever. More puzzle pieces were added, some taken away . . . and still nothing fit.

Harrick got back to Lansing about 6:30 that evening. He decided to hang onto the cruiser and exchange it back for his car in the morning. As he pulled into his driveway he noticed Amy's car parked to one side. He pulled up next to hers and turned the car off.

Amy had a dorm room on the Michigan State Campus on the East Side, but it was not unusual for her to stop by the house to do laundry, have a meal or just hang out. Harrick kept her bedroom the way it was when she lived here, and occasionally, it got used when she worked late or her dorm roommate was "entertaining" for the weekend.

Harrick walked up to the front door and put his key in the lock. Before he opened the door, he rang the doorbell 3 times about a second apart. It was a signal he used to tell whoever was inside, beginning with Amy's mother when she lived there, that it was he who was coming into the house through the front door. Both Amy's mom and Amy knew where the 12 gauge pump shotgun was hidden, and Amy knew how to use it.

"Amy!?" Harrick shouted as he came into the living room. He could see lights on in the kitchen and smelled . . . spaghetti sauce?

No answer.

"Amy!?" he shouted a second time.

Amy shouted back from the laundry room. "Back here. Doing laundry."

Harrick relaxed and walked back to the kitchen. Amy came in with arms full of clothes, fresh from the dryer. He heard another load in the washer turning through another cycle. Amy dropped the load on the kitchen table, which was customary for her, then sat down and started folding.

"Can you turn up the heat on the pot of water, Pops? I didn't know when you would be home."

"Laundry night?"

"Yah." Amy looked up and grinned, "Thanks Pop."

Harrick turned the heat up under the pot of water on the stove. A pot of Prego spaghetti sauce was simmering on another burner.

Harrick grabbed a Vernors out of the refrigerator. He turned toward Amy. "Want one?"

"A water please."

He got a bottle of water and brought them to the table. Harrick set the water near Amy and sat down.

"We heard about your car at work. Got lucky."

"Yupper, damn lucky."

Amy leaned sideways and pulled a piece of paper out of her jeans pocket. "I talked to Maggie over in burglary and got the name of a different alarm company. Maggie says these guys don't use off the shelf equipment. They build their own. Best around she says and they give a 15% discount to cops. Name and number here." Amy tapped it then handed the paper over.

"Thanks, I'll call them tomorrow."

"You know I think Maggie likes you. You should ask her out."

Harrick thought about that. He wondered if he knew how to date anymore. He had his work, his classic car, Amy, a nice quiet home. What was he really missing anyway?

Amy then set a stack of her folded bikini underwear on the table.

Harrick stared and thought, *Yah. That's what's missing.*

"Okay. Maybe. After I solve this case . . . maybe."

Amy looked up and smiled.

"And you?" Harrick added. "What about that football star you were dating?"

"Second stringer. Dropped him. He looked great but dumb as a rock. How's the case going?" Amy asked, quickly changing the subject.

Harrick filled her in on his day in Southfield. When he finished, he noticed the water was now boiling. He went over to the stove, broke a good portion of spaghetti in two, and dropped it into the water. He stirred the pot a few times then set the timer.

"So what did you find at the house?" Amy was now folding his boxer shorts, which, along with her intimate apparel on the table, slightly embarrassed him.

"Like the Barnes' house. Large, upper middle class. Lots of places for a good thief to approach and not be seen."

"But not a thief!" Amy added.

"Right, not a thief. Something personal. Someone with skills. Former military probably. Someone who has a job that moves him around or gives him the time off to do these." He sipped at his beverage.

Amy paused from her laundry and looked up. "I ran every possible program we have so far and can't find anything that connects the 3 of them."

"Maybe there isn't. Maybe it's just coincidence. We have to consider that."

"What does your gut tell you Pop?"

Harrick paused, stared at his soda can and thought before answering. "That these are not just coincidences, kid."

The timer went off and Harrick checked. The spaghetti needed just a little more boiling time. Soon Amy had the table cleared and the clothes in respective his and hers baskets.

"Did you add the sugar?" Harrick asked. Harrick's first wife taught him the trick of adding a little sugar to the sauce. It took out the sharp acid tangy taste of the sauce and smoothed the flavor out. He later learned that some people add chocolate for the same reason, but he stuck with the sugar.

"Of course," Amy replied.

Part way through dinner Amy asked the obvious question. "What's next?"

"Cadillac."

CHAPTER 17

H arrick discussed with Captain Meyers the findings from the trip to Southfield. Meyers agreed that more pieces of the puzzle might be in Cadillac. Meyers called ahead to the Cadillac Post and informed Captain Summers, the post commander. He also called Sheriff Starr and let her know that Harrick was coming, and why. Harrick spent a couple of days clearing some minor things off his desk and on Thursday headed up-state.

He picked up an unmarked black SUV at the motor pool. Amy and one of her lab friends would drop his car back at his house. Amy was staying there and was going to let the new security company in to rewire the house while he was away. "Just don't pick a code too complicated for my old brain," he had pretended to plead.

Harrick threw his hotel bag in the back seat and caught US-127 North out of Lansing. At Clare he thought for a moment of stopping at the very large Jay's Sporting Goods to see what was new in fishing gear, but decided to wait until the trip back. Instead he turned onto Michigan 115 North for the rest of the trip to Cadillac. Michigan 115 was a 2 lane road, a little slower, but Harrick enjoyed the scenery.

In a few hours he was checking into the Days Inn in Cadillac. He had stayed here before and they honored the "state rate," for which he would be reimbursed. He showed his badge and requested a ground floor room which he preferred.

Harrick had spent 5 years assigned to the nearby Gaylord Post as a trooper. He knew his way around the northern lower peninsula and the major towns- Cadillac, Traverse City on the west and Alpena on the east. Captain Summers knew Harrick from when Jim was stationed in Gaylord. They were good friends and fishing buddies.

After a quick unpacking he drove over to the Cadillac State Police Post. It was about 11:30 when Harrick checked in at the front desk and was waved back to Summers' office. "He's expecting you," said the desk jockey.

"How the hell are you Jim?" Summers smiled a big grin when Harrick walked in.

"Hungry Bob. Let's go to lunch."

Harrick had on a light brown sports coat, long-sleeved shirt and khaki pants. Captain Summers was dressed, as usual, in a Michigan State Police uniform. They shook hands vigorously, as friends do. Summers grabbed his service hat and ushered Harrick out the door.

Summers drove and they stopped at a small diner downtown. Summers, who knew the menu by heart, ordered a meatloaf sandwich and coffee.

"Meatloaf any good?" Harrick asked.

"Best around!"

On such a hearty recommendation, Harrick got the same and a Coke.

When their drinks were served, Summers started the conversation. "How's Amy?"

"She's doing great. She is working part-time at the lab while she's going to MSU."

"Go Green!" Summers exclaimed.

"How's June and the boys?" Harrick asked.

"All doing great. Tom may get a swimming scholarship at MSU or Central. Doing any fishing down there?"

"No, very little. It's one of the things about being in Lansing. There just isn't the outdoorsy stuff like up here." Harrick added, "I've thought of taking a demotion and coming back up. Any openings in your house?"

Summers sipped his coffee. "You may think you want to come back up but wait until you're retired. You love what you're doing now and you're damn good at it."

"Maybe, at least, I should buy something up here. A place to spend some of my vacation time."

"Well," Summers responded, "I know of some lots on Lake Missaukee that just came on the market. Thinking of one myself. I'll put you in touch with the realtor. She's the wife of one of my troopers."

Harrick thought that might be a good idea. An expensive idea maybe, but a good one. "Thanks!"

The waitress brought their lunch and refilled Summers' coffee. "I'll be right back with another Coke for you hun," she said in a sing-song voice.

Harrick asked, "So what do you know of the Lisowski murders?"

"Not much. Still unsolved. Sheriff Starr and the county did the initial investigation. It's in their territory and no reason at that time for us to get involved."

"They didn't ask for help?"

"No. They're pretty good here." Summers added, "They have a competent coroner and a decent but limited lab."

"And Sheriff Starr? That was a big change."

"Ya, Potter hit it big. First person I ever knew that won. I'm sure he is enjoying himself in St. Thomas. He's invited us down. Says the fishing is great."

"How did Starr get elected? Wasn't Deputy Sheriff Cooper next in line?"

Summers put down his fork and drank some more coffee. "Big scandal up here about 7 years ago. You remember how Potter got the job?"

"Sure, big Federal Drug Enforcement/Treasury sting. Found the sheriff and some of his deputies involved in drug running and money laundering. Only a few in the state police knew of the investigation."

"So," Summers added, "the sheriff and some top deputies go to jail. Potter is the highest ranking deputy left and is temporally appointed sheriff. He runs next election and wins, as he does the next 4 years. People in town thought Cooper might have been involved but there was no proof. Deputy Starr transferred up from Detroit PD at about that time. She's a good officer, smart and very likeable. She moved up fast in the department and when Potter resigned the party elite decided that Starr was a better candidate than Cooper."

"How did Cooper take it?"

"Cooper wasn't happy but he had 20 years in at that time. Starr likes him and kept him on; so Chief Deputy Sheriff Cooper went over well enough. I think Cooper decided that he should just get in his 30 and retire."

"Dessert fellows?" The waitress had popped back over.

"Not for me," Harrick said, "And by the way, this was excellent meatloaf."

"Breakfast of champions!" she said as she dropped the bill on the table and picked up their cleaned plates.

Summers grabbed the bill, "My treat."

"But I'm on expenses!"

"So you are, so you are." A smiling Summers handed the bill over.

CHAPTER 18

Harrick drove over to the Wexford County Sheriff's Department. At the front desk he identified himself and said the sheriff was expecting him. The officer on duty picked up a phone, dialed a 2 digit extension, and spoke for just a few seconds. "She'll be right out." He nodded towards some chairs.

The inter office door opened and Sheriff Elinor Starr walked out. The sheriff was an attractive lady in her mid 40s, Harrick guessed. She was wearing the usual brown uniform of county sheriff departments as opposed to the blue uniforms of the Michigan State Police. Many years ago, the vendors of officer uniforms had started making them for the female frame. Harrick observed that Sheriff Starr fit nicely in her uniform. The leather industry followed suit and made the holster/utility belts tapered for ladies, as opposed to the straight belts the men wore. A Glock 19 was on her duty belt.

"Good afternoon, Detective Harrick. Welcome to Wexford County." Starr extended a hand. "I know you've been here before so I'll skip the 10 cent tour."

Harrick shook hands, a firm confident grip he noticed. "Good afternoon sheriff. Thanks."

"Let's go back to my office. I want to bring in Chief Deputy Steven Cooper. He's been working on it. "

As they walked back, Starr popped her head into an open office door. "Cooper? Harrick's here. Come on back."

Starr's office was reasonably sized and furnished. Harrick chose a comfortable looking leather chair, one of a matched set in front of Starr's desk. Deputy Cooper came in and they exchanged pleasantries.

"So, give me the cop to cop version of the Lisowski killings," Harrick asked.

Starr nodded to Cooper who spoke up. "About 4 years ago, in April 2012, Lisowski comes home from work and finds his family clubbed to death. I know you have the file so I won't go into the details of the deaths. Suffice it to say someone was really pissed off." Jim nodded.

"Of course we figured it was Stan first," Cooper continued, "but he had a rock solid alibi and there was zero indication of marital troubles. We've gone cold on this."

"Are there any other suspects?" Harrick asked.

"A few sniffs, disgruntled past coworkers, etc. but nothing current to the crime. We still followed up tips but they've led nowhere."

"I would like to see the crime scene," Harrick stated.

Starr answered, "Not much to see, our team went all over it at the time."

"No offense sheriff. From the report I know your team did an excellent job in covering the area. I just want to get a feel for the location."

"No offense taken detective, and thanks for the compliment. There is a new family in it now. I'm sure there will be no problem for a walk around. I'll call them this afternoon to get permission."

"That would be great."

"Where are you staying?" Starr asked. "I can pick you up in the morning about 9 if that's okay?"

"Sure. Days Inn. See you at nine."

~ ~ ~

The assassin was also planning, now that a state police detective was in town nosing around. The schedule would have to be moved up. It would not be long before this hot shot from Lansing would put it all together. The weekend would be free for one mission. The other would have to wait.

CHAPTER 19

Harrick's alarm went off at 7:30. He took a quick shower and dressed in his usual light, short sleeved, button down shirt and light khaki pants. He clipped his holstered Sig inside the waistband on the right side of his belt. His brown sports coat would cover it and he placed his ID and badge in the inside chest pocket.

Forgoing a jacket right now, he went down to the complimentary breakfast that every hotel seemed to have now. The Days Inn one was better than most. After several cups of coffee, some eggs, potatoes and bacon, Harrick went back to his room.

He checked the time; nearly 8:30. He called Amy to let her know how things were going but mostly as an excuse for checking on her. "Nuttin new," she replied. He would call his boss later in the morning to fill him in.

At 8:55 he went down to the lobby. It was cool out and looked like it would be a pleasant spring day.

Harrick had just arrived when he saw Sheriff Starr pull in driving a white and black Ford Bronco. She smiled and nodded to Harrick as he climbed in.

"Good Morning detective."

"Good Morning."

"The Lisowski place is about 15 miles out. We should be there in 30 minutes. I called the Grangers, the new owners. They said it was okay to walk around outside."

"Can we go in?" Harrick asked.

"Nah, they didn't offer. So unless there is a compelling reason I don't want to press it for now." Starr noticed he had no problem with that so moved on to more casual talk. "You used to work around this area I'm told?"

"Ya, I was assigned to the Gaylord Post for several years. Then with my bad luck they found out I could read & write and they made me a detective. Then they moved my butt from God's Country to Lansing."

Starr laughed at that. She knew the hard work it took to make detective in the Michigan State Police.

"So you have been over here a time or two." Starr stated.

"I've been to the cities Cadillac, Traverse City, Ludington, been fishing on Lake Missaukee, but I don't know the outlying areas that well. Cadillac is a lot different than Detroit," Harrick commented.

"Oh, checking up on me?"

"No, Captain Summers filled me in. I had gone fishing a few times with him, Sheriff Potter and a mutual friend, when I was working up here. I heard how Potter won it big and moved to the Caribbean. Summers mentioned that you had come from Detroit and made a name for yourself here."

"A good name I hope."

"Yes, a very good name for yourself. Summers thinks you're very good at the job."

"I'll have to send him a Christmas card." Starr smiled. "Yup, long way from Detroit. All I can say is that managerial attitudes are different here than there."

Harrick thought he understood.

Starr turned right off the main road and drove down a paved secondary. After about a half mile, she turned into a driveway and parked. "Here we are."

Harrick stepped out and took the whole view in. The house was a ranch style with an attached garage facing the street. It sat about 100 feet back. There were other homes around but all the lots were big. *Lots of distance between houses,* Harrick noted. Jim walked around to the right side of the house, the garage side, staying at least 20 feet from the structure. There was one window on this side leading into the garage.

"The report said no windows were broken or appeared to be tampered with, including this one?"

"Correct," Starr replied. She didn't mind the redundant question because she knew how detectives processed a crime scene and expected such inquires. They were just thinking out loud and not being critical of previous cop work.

Harrick continued his walk around to the back yard. The back yard was expansive and devoid of trees. A swing set, sand box, bicycles, baseball bat and various children's toys were scattered about.

"Oh. Hi sheriff. Sorry about the mess." A lady appeared at the back door.

"No problem Mrs. Granger. I used to have kids myself. I know how it goes," Starr replied with a smile. "We won't be long."

Harrick remembered in the crime photos that the back yard had been almost empty, sans a boat on a trailer and a clothes line with laundry hanging at the time of the murders. The tree line at the back of the property, probably the property line, was at least 500 feet back.

"Nice piece of land," Harrick remarked.

"Once we cleared Lisowski, he cleared out. Moved to Kansas with his brother and their family. This place sold quickly despite the history."

"Where did he work?" Harrick knew it was in the report but wanted to bring Starr in feeling like an associate.

"Northern Trucking. Small family owned business. They ran about half a dozen dump trucks, hauling mostly gravel and sand for construction sites. He and his older brother Adam owned the company. After the murders, the company went belly up and Stan moved to somewhere in Kansas with Adam and his family."

Starr had provided more information than the report had.

Harrick continued around the house. *Not much cover,* he noted, *but not that near to neighbors either. A person could approach either by front or back and not be noticed by others. Perhaps the victims even knew the killer or killers and let them in.*

Harrick walked back to the front. He recalled the photos of the murder scene in his head and, while looking at the front, reasoned where each room was located. He pictured the central hallway from the kitchen — the kitchen where Mrs. Lisowski had been found on the floor. Then he mentally wandered down the hall, past the door to the master bedroom and down to the bedroom at the end. That was where Lisowski had found Stan Jr. and Josh.

Harrick closed his eyes and thought. *Basket of damp clothes found dropped outside. Mom outside hanging laundry hears screams from the house. She drops the basket and runs in. Meets killer in the kitchen as he comes from bedroom. Doesn't stand a chance as she is hit repeatedly, savagely . . . yes, someone was really pissed off.*

"Harrick?" Starr's voice brought him back. "What you thinking?" she added.

"Mentally reviewing the murder. I think your forensic team got the sequence right. Still very brutal."

"Ya, I thought I had seen it all in Detroit but this gave me nightmares."

They drove back toward town in silence for a little while. Then Starr broke the ice. "It's almost lunch. You like fish?"

"Sure, properly prepared fresh fish is always on my list of good eats."

"There's a family run place near here. Kaufmann's Korner. I think you'll like it, how about some lunch?"

"Sounds good!" Harrick replied while concealing a small grin.

CHAPTER 20

Kaufmann's Korner was a family-run restaurant on Lake Mitchell, just west of Cadillac. Besides the restaurant, they also rented boats, had a few cabins for rent and sold fishing tackle and bait. They used to sell gasoline and work on cars, but when the big name stations came to town many years back, they couldn't compete with them, so they cut back to what they did best.

Sheriff Starr pulled the Bronco up to the main entrance. The majority of the lunch crowd hadn't arrived as yet.

Harrick walked in first and after a few feet, froze.

"I thought they locked you up for impersonating a champion fisherman!" Harrick was staring at a tall man walking with a limp coming toward him.

"I should have drowned you the first time you spilled us all and we lost that half case of beer!"

Harrick and Ken Kaufmann got nose to nose. Then they broke into smiles and threw their arms around each other.

Ken spoke first. "Jim, you son of a bitch, why didn't you tell me you were coming up? We still have fish in this lake."

"Sorry Ken. Last minute plan. Up here on some work, but I was going to stop by eventually."

"The mutual friend, I assume," Starr said with a smile.

"Bingo Sherlock!" Harrick replied. "Ken and I were in the army together, both doing military police duty. After we got out, we both joined the state police. Following our training at the academy, he was sent to Grand Rapids and me first to Lansing, then Gaylord. A few years later, Ken got transferred up to Gaylord and we have been lying about fish we almost caught ever since."

"And the half case of beer?" Starr asked.

"That wasn't totally my fault if I remember correctly," Harrick said. "Seems alcohol was involved, a storm and a very rough lake at the time . . ."

"Let's stop with alcohol involved all around," Ken interjected with a smile.

"Jim!" Ken's wife Polly, coffee pot in hand, came over and hugged Harrick. "You in town long?"

"Probably a couple of days."

"Well stay the weekend and take this old man fishing." She pushed a finger into Ken. "You can stay in one of the cabins."

"I'd like that. It's a deal."

Starr and Harrick sat in one of the open booths.

Polly came over with a Coke for Harrick and coffee for the sheriff. She didn't have to ask, knowing both well. They had other staff; waitresses, cooks, a busboy . . . but Polly liked to mingle with her customers.

"Some good trout today," Polly stated.

Both Harrick and Starr nodded.

As Polly walked away, Starr asked. "So what's the story with you and Ken? I've been coming here awhile but didn't know he worked for the state police."

"Ken and I have been friends for many years. We've been fishing buddies since he was transferred up to Gaylord. Sometimes Sheriff Potter and Captain Summers would join us. After fishing, we'd play some cards, drink some good whiskey and smoke good cigars. Nothing brings guys together like fishing, drinking and cigars.

One night about seven years ago, Ken was on patrol on I-75 near Vanderbilt and got an officer needs assistance call from the Indian River area. Ken raced up I-75 and, at about Wolverine, a deer came out into the roadway. The deer crashed right through the windshield and Ken lost control. He broke his leg in several places. That's why the limp still shows and he retired on full disability. The officer up in Indian River is okay. Others came to his aid.

So Ken came over to the family restaurant and started working here. A few years back, his parents retired to Arizona and gave Ken and Polly Kaufmann's Korner. Ken is also part of my vintage car group and has several nice automobiles out in that old auto repair building next door."

Polly showed up with two large plates of fish, fries, hushpuppies and coleslaw. Harrick knew there were extra portions here and also knew he had to finish all of it.

That wasn't hard given the quality of the food.

CHAPTER 21

Early morning Sunday found Harrick, Ken Kaufmann and Bob Summers sitting in a fishing boat on Mitchell Lake. They had guided the boat about 500 feet from the Kaufmann's dock to a marshy area that had always been lucky for them. Well, at least in the past. They had been there 45 minutes with just a few nibbles. As usual they had all left their cell phones on shore. This was non-working, non-thinking relaxing time.

"I think you've fished this lake out Ken," Harrick commented.

Ken didn't look back at Jim but just replied, "I haven't been out here in over a year. Must be Bob is just bad luck."

Bob chuckled. "Is it too early to open the beers?"

In the distance they heard a bull horn.

"Detective Harrick! Detective Harrick!"

All three looked up and over to the dock. They could see a white SUV with emergency lights flashing and 2 people standing on the end of the dock.

Ken glanced at Jim with a puzzled look. Harrick just shrugged his shoulders in an I don't know gesture. They reeled in and Ken started the small outboard motor. In a few minutes they were back at the dock. Sheriff Starr and Deputy Sheriff Cooper were waiting.

"I think we got another one," Starr said.

"Where?"

"Traverse City."

"That's in Grand Traverse County, out of your jurisdiction."

"But not yours Harrick. I thought you would want to know as soon as we got the news."

"Go ahead Jim," Ken said.

Summers added, "I'll call the post up there and talk to Sheriff King. Let them know you're coming. Give me details when you can."

"Ride with us?" Starr offered.

"Give me 5 for a quick change."

In 6 minutes Harrick was riding shotgun to Starr. Cooper sat in the back so Starr could fill Harrick in on what she knew. With lights on, they were flying up US 131.

"Sheriff King called me out of courtesy. He knew of our murders here." Starr focused on keeping her eyes straight ahead on the road. "Happened last night. Someone broke in. They clobbered the husband, a Mr. Hughes, and he was knocked out. When he came to, and they think it was only 10 to 15 minutes or so, he finds wife and teenage boy stabbed repeatedly and laying on the floor. Wife's dead but son is still breathing. Son is in emergency surgery at Burns Hospital. Hughes is there also, in ICU with a concussion."

"Sounds close to ours, but not planned out like the others, too hurried."

"I know," Starr replied. "But Sheriff King thought you should come and look anyway."

After a fast drive, they pulled up to a high-end house on Traverse Bay. There were already a dozen sheriff and state police cars blocking the roadway. They parked a quarter mile down and walked to the scene. Yellow tape had been placed all around the perimeter of the lot. Harrick thought they must have used a couple thousand feet of tape to cover the area.

As they approached the drive, 2 Grand Traverse county deputies and a trooper stopped them.

"Sorry, can't go in," one of the deputies said to them while holding up his hand.

"Good morning deputy," Harrick said while holding up his badge and ID. "I'm Detective Jim Harrick from the Michigan State Police and this is Sheriff Starr and Deputy Sheriff Cooper of the Wexford County Sheriff's Department. I believe Sheriff King is expecting us."

The Grand Traverse deputy stepped away and got on his radio. He walked back to them and told them to go on up. "But don't go off the driveway," he added.

Halfway up the driveway, they were met by Sheriff King.

"Hi King," Starr said.

"Hi Starr, Cooper." Sheriff King nodded. "You must be Detective Harrick."

They shook hands then turned up the driveway.

"I can't let you in or anywhere else around the property right now. We have crime scene investigators still going through the place," King said.

"When did this happen?" Harrick asked.

"About midnight. All we know now is that someone bypassed the alarm and came in. Mr. Hughes heard some noise and got up to investigate. He said he just got past the hallway into the dining room when he was hit from behind. He hadn't turned any lights on so didn't see anything. When he wakes up, he's got a splitting headache. He goes back to the bedroom, turns on the light and finds his wife on the floor. Blood everywhere he says. Next he shouts for his son." King looked at his notebook. "Terry is his name. When Terry doesn't respond, he checks on him and finds him bloodied on his bed, but breathing. Hughes calls 911 and we had people here immediately."

"Can I just look through the doorway?" Harrick asked.

"Sure, but you know the routine, don't touch anything."

Harrick , Starr and Cooper stepped up to the doorway. There were lots of lights on plus the sun was now shining through the several skylights. They saw muddy shoeprints back toward the dining area. "It rained last night," Harrick commented.

"Ya,", Cooper added. "A big thunderstorm came off the lake. We got the tail end of it."

They walked back to the driveway.

Harrick spoke next. "That's really strange."

Cooper responded, "Sure is, was thinking that myself."

"What?" Starr asked.

"The scene is sloppy. Not like the others. Just thinking, either this is not related, or . . ." Harrick trailed off, looking back at the house.

"Or what?"

"Our guy is getting nervous, anxious. He's moving his timetable up. He doesn't care anymore about trying to frame anyone. I'll bet they don't find the knife."

They met up with Sheriff King again.

"Please let us know when the crime scene is done," Starr said.

"Sure, may be a couple of days though," King replied.

Harrick asked King, "Who is this Hughes? What did he do? Any dubious background?"

King looked side to side to see no one was near. "Look, this is off the record and will not be in any preliminary report. Hughes is a specialty attorney in divorce and bankruptcy. Makes big bucks. We hear through the grapevine that he knows how to hide assets, move money around in semi-legal ways. We looked into several complaints over the years but haven't been able to prove anything. All I can tell you now is that some people think, me included, that he is a real snake of an SOB. There will be many people with motives we will have to weed through."

As they walked back to the SUV Harrick said, "Let's go to Burns Hospital. See if Hughes can talk."

CHAPTER 22

They arrived at Burns Clinic during the lunch service chaos. Harrick showed his badge and was waved right into ICU. At one door he saw a Michigan State Trooper standing guard. Bypassing the nurse's station, Harrick walked confidently up to the trooper. Starr and Cooper followed. Harrick showed his gold shield to the trooper who nodded back. The three entered Hughes' room.

Hughes was in bed semi-reclined. His head was bandaged. He had a number of IVs going into him and several monitors near him unrelentingly beeping, indicating Hughes' current state of health.

"Mr. Hughes?" Harrick asked looking down at the man.

Hughes' eyes cracked opened slowly.

"I'm Detective Harrick of the Michigan State Police. I would like to ask you a couple of questions."

"Already . . . answered . . . all I could," Hughes replied.

"I know, I'm sorry. You didn't see anyone?"

"No . . . just walked out then . . . on the floor. How's my son?"

"Still in surgery." Harrick supposed. "I'm sure someone will be in as soon as they know."

A nurse entered. "Who are you? You didn't check in did you?!"

"No, sorry, I'm Detective Harrick of the Michigan State Police."

"Well, you must leave. Talk to Doctor Bronson if you want to come back."

"Thank you, we will," Harrick said with a big disarming smile.

As they were leaving, Harrick turned back toward Hughes. "Just one more question please. Did you do any work for Northern Trucking or the Lisowski Brothers?"

Hughes eyes opened wide. "I don't have to tell you who any of my clients were or weren't!"

As they walked to the SUV Starr asked, "What was that all about?"

"I think this whole thing revolves around Northern Trucking. Stan Lisowski, part owner, has his family murdered. Then Northern Trucking goes bankrupt. Hughes is a bankruptcy attorney who is good at hiding assets. But *for what* is the next question."

"But Hughes didn't say that they were clients of his."

"Oh but he did. He used the words 'I don't have to tell you who any of my clients *were* not *are* when he invoked client attorney privilege."

Harrick looked Starr in the eyes, then continued. "Let's meet tomorrow if that's okay and go over the Lisowski file together. I want to try to find Adam Lisowski – hopefully he's still in Topeka."

"Ya, that is where he moved, last we heard."

~ ~ ~

The assassin got back early morning. Hiding the white compact car back in the garage, the assassin knew he would not use it again. Quickly the wet muddy clothes came off and a work uniform took their place. Late for his shift a few hours but he'd claim a flat tire and flat spare. Charlie would have clocked both of them in anyway. They did that for each other.

Sloppy. If I only had more time to plan. But fuck, that's done and the last one won't be hard.

CHAPTER 23

Monday morning Harrick packed up from his cabin and moved back to the Days Inn. He called his boss and filled him in on the Traverse City murders. "I have some ideas," Harrick told him. Captain Meyers agreed and told him to stay there awhile. He made a quick call to Amy then headed over to the state police.

He checked in and knocked on Captain Summers' open door.

"Come in Jim. Have a seat. Need some coffee?"

"No, had my share with breakfast at the Days Inn."

"Heard the details of the Traverse City murders. Any connection?"

"I think so. Hey, I need your interdepartmental communications officer to contact Topeka, Kansas for me."

"Sure, this way." He led Harrick down the hall to another office.

"Greg, this is Detective Harrick. He needs to talk to Topeka PD."

"I need to ask them if they have any information, good or bad, on an Adam Lisowski."

Harrick turned to Summers. "If I can borrow an office, Greg can direct the call there."

"No, direct it to my office please Greg." Turning back to Harrick, he explained, "You can catch me up on things while I do paperwork."

In 15 minutes the phone rang. Summers answered. Greg was on the other end. "I've got Chief Robinson, Topeka PD on the line."

"OK, thanks, put him on."

"Want this private Jim?"

"No, speaker is OK."

Summers pushed the correct button and Harrick spoke. "Hello? Chief Robinson?"

"Yes, this is Robinson."

"Hi, I'm Detective Harrick , Michigan State Police and with me is Captain Summers, Michigan State Police Cadillac Post commander." Harrick shifted around the desk so he was speaking directly into the phone. "Listen. We didn't mean to bother you to return our call. I'm just looking for one of your staff that can find out some background on a Mr. Adam Lisowski. They can get back to us later."

"No need to get back later," Chief Robinson said. "That's an infamous name here."

"Why so?" Summers injected.

"Two and a half years ago Mr. Lisowski came home and said he found his wife and 2 children murdered. Pretty brutal. They had been having marital troubles for a while, and many said he had a mean temper. There was some circumstantial evidence that he did it. His alibi was a girlfriend he was screwing. But he got a hung jury at trial."

"You're talking about Adam Lisowski, not his brother Stan aren't you?"

"Yes, Adam. His brother was here for a couple years but took off before the murders. We don't know where he is. If you find him, we would like to talk to him."

Harrick asked about the date, time and details of the murders. "One more question chief," Harrick asked. "Did the Lisowskis seem destitute to you?"

"No, they seemed very well off. They had a large house, great neighborhood and he moved his parents into a smaller bungalow on the property. The parents were in Hawaii at the time of the murders. "

"Thanks, chief."

"You're welcome. If you got something there to nail this creep, I'll be happy to help."

After the call ended, Summers spoke. "What does that tell you?"

"Maybe that Hughes was employed to hide assets. But I don't know why yet."

CHAPTER 24

Harrick arrived at the sheriff's office about 11:00am. Sheriff Starr and Deputy Cooper were already in the conference room. They had the Lisowski murder file laid out on the conference table.

Harrick informed Starr and Cooper what he had learned from Topeka. They all agreed that it looked like the same guy.

"I read through this a while back but let me ask some questions. What happened to Northern Trucking 8 years ago when they went bankrupt?"

"Not sure," Starr replied. "Cooper, that was a little before I came on here. You know more than I do."

"Well, let's see." Cooper was deep in thought. "They seemed to be doing well. Then there was that terrible accident, and 6 months or so after that, they went under."

"Accident?" Harrick asked. This was not in the report.

"Ya. One of their drivers, Otis Green, ran a stop sign and T-boned a small car. He had a full load and just destroyed that little thing. Unfortunately a young mom and her son were inside. Both died instantly. Otis had been drinking, as he was known to do. Blew double the legal limit. He got convicted of vehicular homicide. Sentenced to 10 years, but just got out in 6 and a half."

"Who were they, the victims?"

"Kate and Hayward Franklin Jr. The boy was 6."

"Father?"

"Hayward Franklin, serving in Iraq at the time. Came home on emergency leave. Buried his family and then filed a lawsuit against Northern Trucking. By the time the lawsuit was filed, Northern had already filed for bankruptcy. There was no money."

"Where is Franklin now?"

"He left the military and now works for the Cadillac Fire Department as a fireman/paramedic."

"Doesn't he sound like a prime suspect in the Lisowski murders?"

Starr spoke up. "Yes, we thought so too at the time, but when we checked with his station he was working that day and night. The chief confirmed it. No way he could have disappeared for several hours and come back unnoticed."

"You know the fire chief well?" Harrick asked Starr.

"Sure, very well. He helped on my election committee."

"Can you get him on the phone?"

Starr made the call and put the phone on speaker. "Tom, Elinor here. Got a minute?" Starr introduced Detective Harrick.

"Chief, if you can do this quietly, can you look up the work schedule of a Hayward Franklin?"

Starr interjected, "He is at the South Station Tom."

"OK, no problem. What do you need exactly?" the chief replied.

"Dates and hours worked," Harrick said. "Take down these dates." Harrick mumbled, looking through his notebook, then giving the chief all the dates of the murders, including Topeka. "I need to know if he was working or not working on those dates. Also for a few days before and after."

"It will take me a while, especially if you don't want people around here to know I'm looking. Give me a couple days."

Starr spoke, "I don't know if we have a couple days Tom. Can't tell you why but, please, it's very important. Please email me your findings as soon as you can to me here at the office. And keep it hush hush."

"OK, I'll get right on it."

"Thanks Tom."

Harrick checked the clock on the wall. "It's lunch time. I need to stop over to Kaufmann's Korner. I left my phone charger there."

"Let's all go over," Starr suggested. "We can talk while we have lunch."

"OK. I'll meet you there."

~ ~ ~

They settled into one of the booths and ordered. Polly brought them their drinks and, coffee pot in hand, stopped by the other tables to fill cups.

Harrick started. "We know that the Lisowski brothers are tied to Northern Trucking. Probably Hughes also. But where do Garcia and Barnes come in? Barnes had a business up here. Did he have any connection to Northern Trucking?"

A female voice came from the booth behind him. "Ted Barnes? He was their accountant."

Harrick leaned back and looked over his seat. "Miss?" he asked.

"Oh, sorry, didn't mean to butt in. But you did ask the question."

"And you are?"

"Mrs. Betty Goodheart. I'm the second grade teacher here."

Polly came over. "Betty, that's right. You used to work for Northern one summer."

"Yupper. Just before I got my teaching certificate. Answering phones, filing and printing invoices mainly. Did it one summer. Then I got the teaching job."

"Oh, Betty," Polly added, "this is Detective Jim Harrick of the Michigan State Police. He's working a case up here."

"Nice to meet you Detective Harrick!"

Harrick got up and came around to Betty. "So you were saying about Ted Barnes?"

"Yes, Barnes was the accountant for the Lisowskis. I think they were one of his biggest clients. He did both the business and each of the brother's personal accounts. It was a small office and I overheard a lot. Not that I'm a snoop mind you."

"Were you there when their truck driver hit that lady?"

"No, that happened about a year after I left. Although I did tell the county prosecutor how Stan and Adam had discussed Otis's drinking problems while I was there. Otis is a cousin or some other relative. I think that's why they kept him on."

Harrick returned and sat with Starr and Cooper. "Did the prosecutor think about charging the brothers with accessory to the homicides if the brothers knew of Otis's drinking problems?"

Starr looked at Cooper for an answer. Cooper stared at the ceiling for a moment, deep in thought. "That was what, 8 years ago? We've changed prosecutors twice since then. I don't know what the prosecutor was thinking then. And he's long gone."

"If Otis Green is involved then he may be next. We should try to find him right away."

"That's not going to be hard," Cooper commented. "Otis is sleeping one off in our county jail right now."

"Well, please keep him there and let me know when he is sober enough to talk to."

"Will do!"

CHAPTER 25

Harrick returned to his hotel room and placed a call to Amy.

"What's up Pops?"

"Got a research job for you. Need info on a person."

"Okay, that's easy. Who?"

"Hayward Franklin. Former military. Now working for the Cadillac Fire Department."

"How deep?"

"See what pops up. If something looks interesting, pursue it."

"Okay, Pops. I've got assignments today but I can get it done tomorrow."

"Early afternoon tomorrow would be good."

Harrick laid back on the bed. He hadn't gotten much sleep last night, so a quick nap was in order. He glanced at the clock on the nightstand, 2:10pm. A couple hours sleep would be good.

~ ~ ~

Harrick opened his eyes. It was dark outside. *What time is it?* 8:23pm the clock told him. "Damn!"

He turned on a light and found his pants. Getting dressed he called the sheriffs' office. "Deputy Cooper please."

"Deputy Cooper just left. Can I take a message?"

"This is Harrick from the state police. Is the sheriff in?"

"No sir, she left a couple of hours ago."

"Can you contact her and have her call me. It's important." Harrick gave the officer on duty his cell phone number.

In 20 minutes the phone rang. "Harrick, what's going on?"

"I fell asleep. I meant to get back over to talk to Mr. Green earlier. I called the station but Cooper had left. Is Green still there?"

"I'll check and get back to you."

Starr returned the call almost instantly. "Green bailed out. They told me Cooper tried to make him stay but Green wanted to go home. Cooper drove him and said he'd check around the house."

"Okay, should we have someone watch the house tonight?

"I don't think so. Green just got out of prison. No one outside of us knows where he's living right now. How about we talk to Green then?"

"Right, pick me up at the Days Inn about 8, if you would please."

~ ~ ~

Otis Green lived in a shack of a house in the country. The small house was probably built in the 1920s, maybe earlier. It was in much need of repair, but demolition would have been cheaper. It was late but Otis didn't have a clock or watch. It was sober time or non-sober time to him.

Otis was a small, frail man. He looked like he was 60+ even though 50 was his real age. Years of drinking and 6 years in prison had taken a toll on his body.

There was a knock at the door. Surprised that someone would venture out this way, Otis nervously looked out the front window. Seeing who it was, he relaxed and opened the door.

"Oh, it's you. Checking up on me?"

"Just wanted to make sure you were safe. Can we talk?" The individual held up a bottle of Wild Turkey.

"Hey, the good stuff. Sure, come in!"

Otis was already two sheets to the wind.

Once in the living room area, the guest cracked open the bottle of whiskey and drank from the bottle. Or at least appeared to drink. Then the guest handed it over to Otis who took a big long swig.

"Hey, you got any glasses?" the guest asked.

"Right this way." Otis turned, almost falling over and headed for the small kitchen.

Once Otis was partway through the doorway, the guest stuck out a leg, tripping him. As Otis was falling, a leather gloved hand pushed on the back of Otis' head, slamming the front of Otis's head into the corner of the metal kitchen table.

Otis twisted in a spasm of pain, falling face up on the kitchen floor. His eyes were open but staring at nothing. Blood was running out of a gash on his forehead. His body twitched a few time, then stopped. The blood flow stopped as soon as the heart stopped.

The guest checked for a pulse. Finding none, glancing around, the killer spotted a small rug in the kitchen and moved it to the doorway, bunching it up a bit. Then left.

CHAPTER 26

S heriff Starr arrived right at 8am. Harrick climbed in the passenger seat and they drove off.

"Otis Green lives about 10 miles from here, a little out in the sticks. I got the address from Cooper this morning," Starr stated.

"People in Detroit would say Cadillac was the sticks."

Starr laughed. "Ya. Probably they would, but most have never been up here."

"Have you heard from the fire chief yet?"

"No, but Cooper is monitoring my account and will let us know when something comes in."

After a slow and winding drive they arrived in front of Otis's home and pulled up into the driveway. An old Chevy pickup truck was parked next to the house.

Starr climbed up to the porch and knocked on the door. "Otis, you awake?"

She knocked again harder. No one answered. "He should be home. That's his truck there."

Harrick walked up and looked into the front window. The old drapes didn't offer much privacy. Harrick had seen the inside of many a drunk's house and this one was usual in its clutter. Seeing nothing unusual, he walked to the back door.

Looking into the back door window, he could see the kitchen . . . and a body on the kitchen floor. "Starr! Quick, back here!"

Starr ran back and Harrick pointed at the man on the floor. They tried the door but found it locked. Starr took a step back and gave it a healthy kick. The old door easily gave way. An old slide bolt-lock from the door flew across the kitchen.

Harrick drew his Sig and covered Starr from the doorway. This was Starr's territory and he allowed her to take the lead. She entered the kitchen with her Glock in hand. She paused, looked around and then knelt by the body.

"No pulse. By the dried blood, I'm guessing it happened last night." Starr backed off, called her office and requested the crime lab and a few other deputies. "I'm going to do a quick search of the house to see if there's anyone else."

Starr disappeared into the living room. Harrick heard her try the front door. She returned quickly. "No one else. Bedroom's clear. Front door is locked. Let's go back out and wait for the crime lab people."

~ ~ ~

Two and a half hours later the county coroner and crime lab people had finished their work. Otis's body was loaded into the county van. The coroner walked out, removed some latex gloves and spoke to Starr and Harrick. "Time of death I'd say between 10pm to 1am last night. I can get it closer after the autopsy."

"Cause?" Harrick asked. "Was he murdered?"

"Can't say now but it looks like a simple accident. He trips on a kitchen rug and slams his head on the table corner. There is an empty bottle of whiskey and a half empty bottle on the table. Front door was locked from the inside with a chain; back door you said was locked also. Windows haven't been opened in years. Just bad luck for Mr. Green I'd say."

"Damn!" Harrick exclaimed.

"Ya, damn bad luck," Starr responded.

~ ~ ~

They drove back in silence for the first few miles, then he spoke. "I'd like to interview Franklin. As soon as possible."

Starr replied, "The chiefs' report on Franklin's time sheets should be in shortly. Let's wait for that, and then if there is gold there we can use it when we talk to him. This afternoon at the latest."

Starr dropped Harrick off at the Days Inn where he picked up his car and drove over to the state police post. Harrick informed Summers about his morning then checked his phone. There was a message and file from Amy. Perfect timing.

Harrick opened the file and shared with Summers. "Franklin was in Desert Storm. Army Ranger. He did several tours in the Middle East. Amy got his military file up. Oh . . . lots of redactions. Has dates, but not details."

"Covert Ops?" Summers asked.

"Ya, that's usually the case with this much empty information. He got a general discharge in 2007 for trauma."

"Something on the battlefield?"

"No, probably the fact that his wife and child were killed that year." Harrick explained the accident to Summers. Harrick looked at his watch, just past 1, and he called Starr on her cell phone. "Have you heard from the chief?"

"Yes, was just ready to call you," Starr replied. "I'm down near the south county line right now but Cooper called me. He said that in the chief's report Franklin was working every time there was a murder. No doubt."

Harrick was silent, thinking.

"Harrick? You still there?"

"Ya, just doesn't make sense. Let's see if we can get together with the chief and go over those timesheets. There has to be a mistake. I'm sure Franklin's our killer."

"The chief is pretty thorough and honest. He wouldn't be covering for him."

"Well, let's talk to him anyway, as soon as possible."

CHAPTER 27

It was late afternoon and Harrick hadn't heard back from Starr. He had Franklin's address and thought about getting a couple of troopers from the post to accompany him to Franklin's house. Instead, Harrick drove out to Kauffmann's Korner for dinner. He wanted to run it all past Ken first.

Harrick was finishing up dinner when he asked Ken if he had a minute to brainstorm. They went to a secluded part of the restaurant, sat down with a couple of beers and Harrick laid out the story. Then Harrick summarized the facts and related the case for Franklin.

"Guy's family's killed. He's overseas doing dirty deeds for our government. He comes right home when he's notified finds that the guy responsible has a history of drunk driving and the company knows about it. The driver is the only one charged and gets 10 years, but is out in 6 ½.

He buries his wife and kid then sues the company. The company, Northern Trucking, goes bankrupt and has no assets. It appears that a shifty attorney worked with the owners and their accountant to hide their assets.

Now this guy is really pissed. He has all the skills needed to pull these murders off. The sheriff interviews him for the first murder but finds he has a good alibi. He now works for the local fire department and has a 5 day on, 3 day off schedule. But we are told he was working the time of the murder. And then, on the dates the other murders happened we find again, he was working during all of them.

"Forged timesheets?" Ken asked.

"Could be. We're going to double check them in the morning."

"The case in Southfield, Jim. Where does that fit?"

"That's another strange thing Ken. It doesn't fit the other murders. Amy checked deep and there is no connection we can find."

"Copycat?"

"I don't think so."

They sat and sipped their beers a few minutes.

"You know what's odd?" Ken murmured.

"What?"

"You have had 5 murders over what, 5, 6 years?" Ken questioned. "And Franklin is working *every* time. Here is a guy who works 5 days on, then 3 off, always rotating, different days on different weeks, and he is fortunate enough to be working the exact dates every time?"

Harrick thought for a moment, then nodded. "Do you have the fire chief's number?"

Ken pulled out his phone and in a minute he had the chief on the line.

"Chief," Harrick said, "I'm Detective Harrick. You talked to me and Sheriff Starr yesterday."

"Sure Detective. What can I do for you?"

"The report you sent to the sheriff on Hayward Franklin's time. Could the timesheets have been altered?"

"Except for the first one. The others were all good."

"First one?" Harrick asked.

"Yes, the date from the first murder. It looked like someone signed in for him. That was in the report."

"But he was working all the other days?"

The chief paused.

"Chief?"

"You didn't see the report Harrick?"

"No, just got a verbal on it."

"I confirmed that Hayward Franklin was off all the days of the other murders."

Harrick froze. *What the fuck?* "One more question chief. Was Franklin working last night?" Harrick listened. "Thanks chief." He hung up Ken's phone and grabbing his own, dialed Starr.

"Sheriff Starr."

"Starr, it's Harrick. Franklin's our guy. Revenge for his wife and child. You got wrong info about his time sheet from the chief's report. He was off those days.

Listen. I'm going out to his house now. He may flee, thinking he's all finished, unless you can think of any others he needs to kill."

She cleared her throat, thinking. "No, can't think of any."

"I'm going to call the post and have a SWAT team stand by. Meet me at Franklin's as soon as you can and leave Cooper out of the loop."

"Okay," Starr responded. "I'm still down on the county line but I can be up there with a dozen deputies in about an hour, hour and a half. Observe but don't attempt to apprehend. Stay back from his drive and wait until we arrive."

CHAPTER 28

Harrick checked his watch: 10:12. It was just 15 minutes since he'd talked to Sheriff Starr. He was parked 200 feet or so from Franklin's driveway. His iPhone App for maps had gotten him this close. He didn't want to get any closer for now. An almost full moon lit up the sky and the surrounding area. Harrick had cut his lights a half mile back and crept up to this present spot. He could just see the flicker of lights coming from Franklin's cabin and guessed Franklin was home.

A small branch hit his front windshield and partially blocked his view. Harrick tossed his cell phone on the passenger's seat and opened the door to remove the obstruction. *Damn wind,* he thought.

Harrick had just grabbed the branch with his right hand when his head was slammed sidewise into the door frame. Stunned, he turned and got his left arm up to block a straight right from Franklin. He did not see the follow up left that caught him in the jaw, knocking him out.

~ ~ ~

Harrick's reality was slowly coming back. Both hands were handcuffed behind his back with his own cuffs. His feet were tied together with cord just above the ankles.

His mind felt like he was halfway asleep/half awake and he couldn't comprehend his surroundings. He was being dragged, feet first. He felt his head hitting board after board on a rough floor, and it didn't make sense to him. It was dark but the area was dimly lit. *I'm outside,* he told himself. He smelled the familiar smell of a lake and heard water gently lapping against something.

As his mind became clearer, he knew he was being dragged down a dock. Franklin stopped at the end and rolled Harrick over the edge and into his small fishing boat. Harrick moaned as his head hit the edge and his hip hit a built-in aluminum seat on the way down.

Franklin untied the mooring, climbed in and pushed the boat away from the dock. He saw Harrick's eyes open and knew Harrick was at least partially conscious. Jim could see his own Sig 239 in Franklin's waistband.

Franklin seated himself, facing Harrick in the back, and started to row. Franklin spoke. "I wanted to let you know

I'm very sorry about this. I didn't want to hurt you but I need a few more days. Call it bad luck."

"Why . . . Why the families?" Harrick mumbled out.

Franklin didn't answer, but continued rowing.

"And why kill Otis Green outright?"

Franklin stopped. He looked puzzled. He then turned his head to the right and looked over the lake, looking for . . . answers?

Harrick could see that there was a large concrete block near his feet. A sudden thought brought him to his senses. He knew what was going to happen. Quickly analyzing his options, and knowing that Franklin seemed distracted, he did the only thing he could think of to save his life.

Harrick gave a strong push with his feet against the seat and pushed himself overboard.

The cold water hit him like a massive blow to the body. He started to sink and found bottom over 8 feet down. He had to get to his hidden tool. Harrick had never done this underwater and his sports coat was tangling his arms.

"*Calm,*" his mind told him. "*Air,*" his lungs said.

He was finally able to push the back of his coat out of the way and his fingers fumbled for the key.

"*AIR,*" his lungs were insisting now. "*CALM,*" he told himself again.

He got the key and un-cuffed one hand. With his legs still tied he was able to kick and stroke with his arms toward the surface.

"*AIR!*" his lungs were screaming.

Harrick broke the surface. He inhaled in a large breath of sweet cold air. He looked around for Franklin.

Franklin was standing in his boat not more than 5 feet away. They caught sight of each other at the same time.

Franklin raised Harrick's pistol. Harrick dove, kicking and clawing at the water trying to get as deep as possible. Shots rang out; 8 – 9 – 10. Franklin emptied the gun at Harrick. Harrick could see the traces of the bullets in the water go past him. He was not deep enough yet. Pain hit him in his left shoulder. He knew at once he'd been hit.

Harrick reached down to his tied legs. When he moved his left arm more pain seared from his shoulder. With a struggle, he was able to free his legs. Still underwater he realized that he had lost his bearings. He had no clue about where the shore was now. But, he had to get away from Franklin's boat.

Harrick was able to swim a good distance underwater from where he thought Franklin would be. He had to surface. On the way up he heard an outboard motor start.

When Harrick surfaced he saw that he had moved parallel to the shore. He was about 20 feet from the dock and at least 30 from the shore. There were some flickers of light dancing in the dark up on the shore. These were flashlights from other lakeside property owners who had heard the shots and were curious as to what was going on. Harrick was lit up by one of them.

He heard a boat motor speed up and looked around. Franklin was bearing down at him full speed, just a few feet away now. Harrick dove again and struck out for the shore. His left shoulder still burned with pain as he struggled for distance.

The boat sped closely overhead and Harrick felt his right foot being struck by something many times in quick succession. More pain struck him like a freight train.

He broke surface, turned and saw Franklin speeding away across the lake. Some of the flashlights followed

Franklin until he disappeared in darkness. Harrick was just a few feet from the end of the dock. People on the dock and shore were lighting him up with their lights.

"Help!" he gasped.

It was a struggle. He was losing consciousness. He was trailing blood fast from his shoulder and foot. He reached out and a hand caught his. Someone pulled him along the side of the dock up to shore. Pulled up on dry land Harrick felt other hands pressing a makeshift bandage against his shoulder. He heard sirens close by getting louder. Red and blue flashing lights lit up the trees above him. People were talking to him but he couldn't focus enough to understand.

Then darkness.

CHAPTER 29

Harrick drifted in and out of consciousness throughout the night. When he was awake, but still groggy, he saw that he was in a hospital room, probably an ICU unit. Machines were lined up beside and above him. He could see various lights, a screen projecting several wave patterns. Numbers flashing, then changing. A pole next to him was feeding an IV into his arm.

His head hurt. His left shoulder hurt. His right foot hurt. They all throbbed and he could not determine which part hurt the worst.

The events of last evening went over and over in his mind. He couldn't shut it off. Franklin was the killer, but that wasn't the whole story. The only way the remaining pieces fit in the puzzle, the only way they could . . . the result not only explained everything, but also chilled him.

A nurse entered his room. He was alone here, no other bed present, which was good. The nurse came over and saw Harrick's eyes open. "Good, you're awake! I'm Nurse Dori and I'm going to be taking care of you this morning. How do you feel Mr. Harrick? Are you in pain?"

Harrick tried to speak but only harsh sounds came from his throat. She took a glass of water with a straw and held it to his lips. After he had a good long drink, the throat cooperated.

"Ya. Pain all over. Head, shoulder, foot."

"On a scale of 1 to 10, with 10 being the worst, how would you describe it?"

"About 8 or 9."

"The doc is making his rounds now and will be right in. We'll see about making you more comfortable." She took his temperature and wrote it down on a metal clipboard. She was checking his IVs when the doctor came in, closing the door behind him.

"Detective Harrick, I'm Doctor Chu. You went through a lot last night. Hit on the head, bullet in your left shoulder, and multiple lacerations to your right foot."

The doctor gave his shoulder a quick exam. "Good news is you were only out a few hours. We need to do a CAT scan on your head. You may have a slight concussion. The bullet went in the back, deflected off your collar bone and went out the front. You have a nick out of your bone but that may grow back and heal over time. Your right foot took a beating, probably from a propeller blade. We see that kind of injury in here every so often. Your heavy duty shoes prevented some nastier deeper cuts. All in all, you have some shallow lacerations which required 26 stitches."

Doctor Chu looked at the chart. "We'll need to keep you here a few more days but if there are no infections or problems from a concussion, such as fainting or dizziness, we can probably get you down to Sparrow Hospital in Lansing for the rest of your recovery. Captain Simmons has been in touch requesting updates on your condition. There are also pair of deputies who've been waiting all night to see you."

Harrick caught the attention of both the doctor and nurse by snapping his fingers. "No. That won't work I'm afraid," Harrick croaked. There was tension, yet firmness in his voice.

"What? Why not?" the doctor queried as they both stared at Jim.

Harrick looked around the sparse room to be sure the door was closed and curtains drawn. "I need a big favor. I need both of you to keep my recovery quiet for a little bit. You can say I'm stable but still unconscious. Say you're concerned about my head wound. I need time. And no visitors until I say so."

"What do you need this time for?" Dr. Chu asked.

"To catch a pair of killers." Harrick nodded to himself as he spoke. "Yes, a pair of killers."

"How much time?" Chu asked.

"Just 24 hours, please give me 24 hours."

Dr. Chu left briefly, then returned, explaining, "I needed to discuss your request with the hospital administrator. She's on board, as well as the head nurse of this section. Don't worry, we're a family here and all can be trusted. I'll tell the officers waiting down the hall you're still out and that I'll contact them if anything changes. Nurse Dori will be assigned to you for the rest of her shift but another nurse will be coming on tonight."

"I'll get Kathi Slack for tonight," Dori said. "She's my daughter."

When the staff logistics were all in place and the doctor had gone, Harrick asked for a phone. "You have a desk phone here on your table." She moved the phone within reach.

"No. I need to borrow your personal cell phone for just one call please."

Dori handed him her phone and he called Ken. Harrick explained what had happened last night, where he presently was, a little about his plan, and a task for him. "Should still be on the front seat of my car, wherever they took it. Only talk to Summers. I'm handing this phone over to a very wonderful nurse who will assist you from this side."

Harrick handed the phone over to Dori and in a couple of minutes they were done.

She left but came back a few minutes later with a syringe. Soon, Harrick was feeling very relaxed.

CHAPTER 30

Shortly after he woke again, Dori came back into the room. "Nothing yet, how's the pain level?" she asked as she gave him another shot

"Better, thanks," he replied.

"That shot should smooth things out for you but not send you into La La Land. You should be good for another 5 hours. But let me know." She filled his water glass and placed it within arm's reach on the side table. "I'll see about getting you some food soon. We can sneak it in so the people waiting to see you won't know you're awake."

"That would be nice," he told her.

When she returned, she made sure the door was closed, curtains drawn, and slipped him his iPhone. "That Mr. Kauffmann is a character," she giggled.

Harrick smiled back as she finished her routine and left the room.

He speed-dialed Amy.

"Hi Pops, what's up?"

Harrick filled her in on last night's excitement, where he was now and his condition.

Amy's first reaction was to say that she was driving right up in a borrowed cruiser. "With lights and sirens, I can make it in under two hours!" she boasted.

"NO!," Harrick hissed. "I need you there. I appreciate the thought kid but get a pen and paper out. I need you to do more research and I need it *quick.* Is the senior tech going to give you any problems?"

"No, Dad, he's off for the day."

Harrick explained to Amy what he needed. "Get back to me as soon as you can, but verify what you find out first."

"Yupper," Amy replied.

"Now, transfer me over to the captain."

Harrick spent the next 20 minutes letting Meyers know his theory and his plan. He needed Meyers to set things in motion from that side.

"How sure are you about this?" Meyers asked.

"Now 99% and will be 99.9% when Amy gets back to me."

CHAPTER 31

The day went by quietly. The nurse was able to bring in a food tray unobserved. For hospital food, it wasn't that bad. Dori told him that the sheriff and a Deputy Cooper stopped in for a few minutes to see how he was doing. They were told Harrick was still unconscious but could come out of it any time.

By what he thought must be early afternoon, Amy called. "Just like you thought. I can't believe it myself. I've PDFd you the report."

"Thanks, sit tight and I'll call you back in a bit."

Harrick downloaded the report and read. Afterwards he set his iPhone in his lap and thought. *The pieces all fit now. How to play it?*

He texted the nurse, and in a few minutes she entered. "Can you get Doctor Chu in here ASAP? I need to talk to both of you."

The nurse left and returned quickly. "Doctor Chu is busy but can be here in about an hour."

"That will work." Harrick called Amy back. "Set up a conference call with Captain Meyers, Captain Summers in Cadillac and yourself, and I'll call you back in about an hour. And brush up on your acting skills."

When Dr. Chu and Dori arrived, Harrick asked them to be patient for a minute while he called Amy.

"I'm in Captain Meyers's office. We have Captain Summers on line also."

"Hi Jim, need some swimming lessons?" Summers chuckled.

"No, I'm staying out of the water for a while, maybe the rest of my life."

Harrick made the introductions then proceeded to lay out his plan. "All of you, and I mean all of you," looking at Dr. Chu and the nurse, "have to be on board. When you consider what they've done, your conscience and moral compass should be very clear."

The doctor and nurse nodded their agreement.

Not long after the conference call, Nurse Dori returned. With her was another nurse, a shorter version of herself.

"Detective Harrick, this is my daughter, Kathi. She will be doing the night shift with you. She's up to date on your plan, and will play along."

"Nice to meet you, Mr. Harrick. Opps, sorry, should I call you detective?"

"No, just Harrick is fine, or Jim even."

"We thought you'd be hungry, so I snuck some food in."
Kathi pulled a large white bag out of her equally large purse.
"Hope you like olive cheeseburgers."
Harrick's afternoon could not have been better.

~ ~ ~

Harrick lay awake until late. He went over his plan again and
again.

Nurse Kathi had given him a half dose of painkiller.

He finally drifted off to sleep.

CHAPTER 32

H arrick's phone rang early in the morning. He looked at the clock and saw 6:45am. The caller ID said Capt. Meyers.

"Rise and shine handsome. It's show time!" Meyers said enthusiastically.

"Gee, thanks captain. What's the news on Franklin?"

"Haven't found him yet. We have FBI and US Border Patrol keeping an eye out. Seems we left Wexford County out of that loop though."

"Gee, darn," Harrick replied.

"All of the assets are in place. You should be getting your visitor very soon."

"Thanks for letting me run with it."

"Good luck Jim."

At 7:15am Nurse Dori entered the room. With her was another, younger nurse. As they approached his bed, the younger nurse's jaw dropped and a frightened look appeared across her face.

"Pops, you look terrible!"

"It's not as bad as it looks Amy. I'll heal right up in no time."

Amy gave her dad a kiss on his cheek and a hug, which pressed against his shoulder.

"Ugh," Harrick grimaced.

Amy brought her hand up to her mouth and teared up. "Sorry Pops."

"It's okay, really. I'm very happy you're here," He said with a big smile. Harrick turned to Dori. "Is Deputy Cooper down the hall?"

"Yes. He's been here all night waiting for a chance to see you. Sheriff Starr has just arrived."

"Amy, do your magic."

Amy first handed him a Ruger LC9 semi auto that was hidden in her nurse's uniform. Harrick tucked it under the sheets. The next steps took a few minutes to set up. Finally, Harrick had them place his phone conspicuously on the table beside him.

As Nurse Dori and Amy were leaving he said, "Send in Sheriff Starr first, please. Tell her I just woke up."

Sheriff Starr stuck her head inside the door. She gave a gentle knock. Harrick looked at her with eyes half-opened and dazed. He weakly signaled her in.

Harrick looked bad. He had a bandage on his head where he had been hit. There was another bandage on his left shoulder where the bullet had passed through. His right leg was elevated and the right foot heavily wrapped.

"Hey Jim. They told me you just woke up. How you feel?"

"Tired . . . sleepy . . . some pain . . . but I think I'm all in one piece. Doc said . . . I did a big scare on them," he mumbled in a drowsy soft voice with eyes that kept drifting shut.

"Yeah, was touch and go I heard." Starr added, "Look, I'm really sorry we didn't get there in time. Why didn't you wait like I told you?"

"Was . . . ambushed. Have you . . . found him yet?"

"No. The boat was found on the other side of the lake. He's on foot so he should still be in the county. He didn't have any close friends that we know of, so no one to help him. He'll turn up."

"He's long gone. In another state . . . maybe out of the country by now."

"How can you be so sure?"

"He had help . . . inside help . . . from your department."

"My department?! Can't be! What makes you think that?"

"He knew. He knew I was outside his house . . . Also he needed information on finding some of his victims. A law enforcement agency . . . " Jim struggled with getting his words out . . . "can do that very easily and without suspicion. Someone tipped him off I was outside his house, watching his only way out."

"Tipped off by whom?"

"Someone in your office. Not a leak . . . but . . . a full-blown accomplice."

"In my office!, NO! CANT BE!"

"That's the only way the pieces of the puzzle fit together." His voice was still staggering, off tempo.

"Who do you think it is?" she demanded.

"Pedro Rivera."

Starr stood silent for a second. Her face went blank, her eyes dead. She was trying desperately to pull her thoughts together. When she spoke her voice had just the slightest quiver. "Who's Rivera? There is no one in my department by that name."

"No,... but you do know him . . . don't you?"

Starr looked around the room and spotted Harrick's phone on the table. She snatched it up, inspected it, and turned it off. A *nice try* stare came from her eyes.

He looked shaken but continued. He had her off balance now with a false sense of confidence and continued in his shaky *I just woke up* voice. "Pedro Rivera is the illegal who ran over your 2 daughters when they were getting off their school bus in Detroit. You watched it happen from the side of the street. Happened in 2008 when you were still an officer on the Detroit PD. It must have been horrible for you to witness. My heart sank just reading about it."

Jim shifted positions with pain running across his face. "Rivera ran but was caught and was booked for vehicular homicide. Antonio Garcia was Rivera's attorney. Garcia convinced a liberal judge in Detroit that witness reports were sketchy and that Rivera at least deserved bail. A hefty bail was granted, posted, and Rivera promptly skipped. He disappeared. I understood the murder connections to Franklin but the Garcia murders didn't fit until now. I suspect that when you transferred up here you met Franklin at a support group maybe?"

Not expecting an answer, he continued, "Anyway, that's when you two became kindred spirits, and plotted your revenge. And then I learned the time sheets didn't match up. The fire chief did his job and sent you the report. But you told me Cooper reported that Franklin was working those days. Cooper never saw that report, did he?"

Starr still stood there, her eyes tearing up.

"What I don't understand is why the families? Why kill them and not the people that ruined both your lives?"

"Have you ever lost a close family member detective?" Starr's voice was quivering. A tear ran from one eye. "A wife, a son or daughter? Have them in your arms one day, telling them how you are going to protect them, to make their world wonderful and safe. Then have them murdered the next moment. And then, then there is no justice? The pain never goes away. It hurts from deep in your gut and never lets up. You can dull it with drugs, alcohol, even sleeping pills. I tried. But it comes right back. You live with the pain the rest of your life. That is the only way Garcia, Barnes, Lisowski and the others will ever, EVER!, understand. Kill their next of kin, their loved ones. They will feel that pain the rest of their lives. And, with Franklin now known as the deliverer of their pain, they will know it was their fault."

"You helped. You are at least an accomplice." Harrick noticed Starr's hand move to her Glock. He tightened his grip on the Ruger under the sheet.

She stood still for a moment, and then seemed to relax. A small smile went across her face. "All circumstantial on me. Besides, Franklin did all the murders."

"Not all of them. It had to be you that killed Otis. Franklin was really at work that evening. When I mentioned to Franklin that Otis was dead, he looked surprised. He didn't know you had already killed him. Otis would have trusted you and let you in. Then, when we were there, you relocked the chain on the front door from the inside, the door you left from the other night."

"I could not have Otis leading you to Franklin, at least not before he could get away. Otis had to go too, but with no family, we couldn't make him feel the pain. Still not enough evidence, especially when the coroner's report states that it was probably an accident. Like you said, Hayward was at work. I couldn't reach him then."

Just then, the door to Harrick's room opened. A doctor and an assistant in long lab coats stepped in.

"Time's up, Sheriff. Detective Harrick really needs to rest. You can come back later."

She smiled at the doctors and placed Harrick's phone back down on the table. "Okay," she told them.

She leaned down and whispered so only Harrick could hear, "Better luck on your next case." She turned and on her way out said, "Get well Jim." She exited and walked down the hall.

When the door was closed, the two doctors removed their white lab coats revealing holstered semi-automatic pistols. They were both wearing bullet proof vests.

"We were within 10 feet the whole time," the first one said. "We heard everything. We got it all taped in the van." One of them removed a hearing device from his ear.

Harrick nodded to the undercover men. He reached over and pulled the bandage off his left shoulder. A small transmitter was taped under that. He removed the transmitter, along with some old growth hairs, and set it on the table. Amy would take it back to the lab in Lansing.

Harrick thanked the 2 troopers and asked them to send Amy and the nurse in. He could use another shot.

If Harrick could have stood up, despite his bad foot, and walked out the door, down the hall, and looked through the large window, he would have seen Sheriff Starr exit the building with Deputy Sheriff Cooper and 2 other deputies. He would have seen the deputies slow their pace and back off, having been briefed when Sheriff Starr was in Harrick's room. He would then have seen a half dozen state troopers, some with rifles at the ready, approach Starr. He would not have been able to hear, but he knew the routine.

She would be given her rights. Starr would slowly raise her hands and a trooper would reach over and remove her gun. Another would remove her utility belt with the holster, cuffs, flashlight, etc. After a pat down, her hands would be handcuffed behind her back and she would be placed in the back of a police car.

CHAPTER 33

FOUR MONTHS LATER

Lieutenant Martinez was just settling in to read the evening paper. He had finished a late dinner with his family and now the kids were off to their rooms. His wife had finished the cleanup and joined him in the living room. She switched on the TV. It was a routine performed most nights. Occasionally, like tonight, the phone interrupted them.

"Lieutenant, this is Sergeant Reyes," said the familiar voice on the other end. "You are needed at 1122 Pino Suarez. A triple homicide."

"Gangs? Drugs?" Martinez inquired. He knew that part of town was not the best area of San Camargo.

"No, looks like a domestic," Reyes replied.

Martinez grabbed his coat and was on his way. He parked a half block down the street. Several San Camargo Policia cars were in front of the residence, their red and blue flashing lights giving a disco dance floor look to the street. An ambulance was parked across the street; the driver and paramedics were leaning against the van smoking cigarettes.

Martinez walked toward the front door. A man in his late 20s was sitting off to the side of the porch with his head buried in his hands. The man was wearing jeans, a dirty Detroit Tiger T-shirt with blood stains and tennis shoes, also with stains. He was sobbing uncontrollably.

Martinez walked past him and found Reyes at the front door.

They nodded to each other and Reyes spoke. "Total of 3 dead. Mom and 2 kids. Looks like all stabbed repeatedly. Found a bloody kitchen knife on the floor just inside the door. Father here," Reyes pointed to the crying man, "said he went drinking after work. Came home about an hour ago. Found them all dead."

Martinez looked into the living room. The coroner was hunched over one of the kids. He saw another in a pool of blood a few feet from the first body.

"Mom is in the kitchen. Same way."

They went back out to the front yard. Reyes pointed again to the man. "He's saying when he came up to the door the knife was just lying there. He didn't see the blood on it in the dark so he picked it up and walked in. He said he dropped it as soon as he saw his children and ran over to them."

"Name?" Martinez asked.

Reyes checked his notes. "Pedro Rivera."

"Okay, take Senior Rivera in. I'll be there in a little while."

Martinez walked back to his car. *Si, probably the father*, he thought.

EPILOG

Elinor Starr was a year into her 20 to life sentence. She had only been convicted of the murder of Otis Green but since more information had come out about her relationship with Franklin, the judge gave her the maximum sentence.

When Starr was arrested, Deputy Cooper ran for Sheriff of Wexford County and won in a special election.

Amy had graduated from Michigan State with honors and was working full-time in the crime lab. She moved into a one bedroom apartment on the west side of Lansing, in Delta Township. She was 5 minutes from her pop's house and occasionally came over for a free meal and to do laundry.

Harrick's Studebaker won best of show a couple of times and placed high in several other car shows.

~ ~ ~

On February 6, 2017, it was a cold morning in Cadillac. The sun was out but the temperature wasn't likely to break 37 degrees. A steady light wind blew in from the west. There was just a trace of frost on the ground.

The man approached the grave sites. He wore a heavy long coat and a knitted hat pulled down over his ears. The ground made crunching noises under his boots. He held a large bouquet of roses in his arms.

He made his way deliberately across the cemetery and stopped in front of a large marker. He knelt down in front of it and wiped away a few flakes of snow.

On the marker was engraved:

Kate Franklin
1983-2007
Loving Wife

Hayward Franklin Jr.
2001-2007
Loving Son

Laying the roses at the base he reached out and put his hand on the headstone. He lingered for several minutes then stood up and put his hands back into his coat pockets. He paused.

"Has the pain lessened? Has it gone away?"

Franklin turned around. Tears were running down his face. He looked surprised.

"The 10th Anniversary," Harrick stated, answering Franklin's unspoken question.

Franklin looked past him and saw a half dozen state troopers, guns at the ready, in a semi-circle about 10 feet behind Harrick.

In a quavering voice Franklin responded, "No, the pain is always there. It never lessens, it never stops, it keeps you awake at night."

"Starr explained the pain to me."

Franklin looked skyward and drew a deep breath. "For what it's worth, I'm glad you survived."

"Any more murders we should know about?"

"Just one in Mexico. Did it for Elinor. She deserved it."

"I'm very sorry for your loss Hayward, but I have to take you in. Please slowly take your hands out of your pockets. Don't make any sudden moves." Harrick had his Sig in his right hand at waist level. His cuffs were in his left hand. He knew the troopers behind him and the SWAT sniper hidden 75 yards away had his back.

Franklin turned toward the gravestone. "You know, this is a family plot." Franklin turned back, "Do me a favor Harrick?"

"I can't promise you anything, Hayward."

"Then a request. Bury me here."

Harrick was close, but not close enough. Franklin pulled a pistol from his pocket, put it to his head and pulled the trigger.

Made in the USA
Coppell, TX
02 July 2023

18700073R00075